The Ties That Bind

ANNIE SEATON

Love Across Time: 4

ANNIE SEATON

This book is a work of fiction. Names, characters, places, magazines and incidents are the product of the author's imagination or are used fictitiously. Any resemblance to actual events, locales, or persons, living or dead, is coincidental.
Copyright © 2022 Annie Seaton

All rights reserved.

ISBN 978-0-6452232-3-1

Dedication

This book is dedicated to my loyal time travel readers, who have been waiting so patiently for this book to arrive!

The other books in the Love Across Time series.

Megan's story: Book 1-*Come Back to Me*

Beth's story: Book 2-*Follow Me*

Lucy's story: Book 3-*Finding Home*

Prologue

Alice's cottage
March - 2019

Beth McLaren leaned back on the feather pillow and chuckled. 'I can't believe I'm in bed with you having a conversation about our visit to the fifteenth century.'

'*I'm* very happy you are in bed with me. Where we belong.'

'You mean *when* we belong.' Happiness filled Beth and she smiled as Silas, her partner, moved closer.

'Yes, exactly. But if you do intend to travel again, we'll be leaving together next time. I'm not going through that again, Beth. But not for a while, please? I'm still getting over the experience.' She looked up at Silas as he shook his head slowly. 'Sometimes I wonder if it was all a dream. Did it really happen? Or was I hallucinating?'

'It did, because if it didn't, we had the same shared dream.' Beth snuggled into his warmth.

'It did happen,' he said quietly. 'The travel over the years to and from the seventies with Davy prepared me for it, but this time? Over five hundred years back. Whoa! It's given me a whole new take on time. I still can't get my head around the past, present and future all being parallel.'

'You and me both! Plus, I agree. If—*when*—we do travel again, we'll leave it for a while. I want to finish reading Alice's diaries, and next time I want to prepare for the visit. The right clothes, something to take note with. The historical research I could do would be amazing if I had a camera that worked when we were back there.'

'Beth, we have to be careful. Davy and I have talked about this often. We don't know if our actions when we go back can change the future. We were always very careful, but we had a couple of scares back in the day. We don't want to find ourselves stuck somewhere we don't want to be.'

'I understand what you're saying. And I have to talk to my mother. A lot of things from my childhood have come back to me. Strange things she said, and other things she avoided talking about over the years. I'm sure she knows about the stones, and I have a feeling that she knows a lot more about Alice than she ever said. I remember Dad saying something once about a "missing bloke" and Mum hushing him. I wondered if maybe Branton came back with Alice some time?'

'After the time we were there?'

'Yes, he was genuinely distressed about her leaving him, so it couldn't have been before then. I wonder if Mum knows anything.' Beth stared at the wall, as she recalled Alice's words. 'There was a child. I think she could have miscarried.'

'Jesus. That's the sort of thing that could change the future. We'll read the diaries, and you call your mum, and then we'll talk to Davy too. Are you happy with that?'

'I am.' Beth snuggled into his bare chest and closed her eyes. 'I wonder if what Mum knows comes from the diaries, or if she knows more. It's supposed to be a family thing. I think back to some of the things Mum's said, and how she tried to stop me reading Alice's diaries and I wonder.'

'You mean, you wonder if she'd travelled through the stones?'

'Yes, but I honestly can't imagine Mum doing that.'

'Why do you say that?'

'It's just not Mum. She's not very adventurous or romantic. She's rigid and very . . . I don't know the right word. You get the gist of what I mean. Always unsettled and often angry.' She pulled a face. 'The only way she would have ever travelled like we did would have been to get away from Dad. And I totally understand that! You'll see what I mean when you meet her.'

'So I'm going to meet your mum, am I? What about your dad?'

'I guess you will if you'll come back to Australia with me when I finally go home.'

'Where you go, I go,' Silas said and pulled her in for a kiss.

'And you've sure proved that.' Beth giggled as his stomach grumbled. 'I don't think we had dinner last night, did we?'

'No, you side-tracked me and dragged me to bed. I'm almost faint with hunger. So, wench, are you going to cook my breakfast?'

'I thought you might cook mine,' Beth said running her fingers up his chest.

'My famous scrambled eggs coming up for you, my love.' Silas climbed out of bed and Beth's eyes lingered on the man she loved; the man who understood her and supported her. The man who had followed her through time.

How many men would come through the centuries to search for you?

He stood beside the bed, and her gaze trailed over the muscular chest, down to that sexy V—A loud knock on the door below interrupted Beth's musing and she sat up straight. 'Who on earth could that be?'

Silas grabbed his jeans and stepped into them before he crossed to the window. He unlatched it and pushed out the swinging window. 'The door's unlocked, man. We'll be down in a minute.' He turned to Beth as he pulled a black T-shirt over his bare chest. 'Looks like we're feeding a few, sweetheart. Davy and Megan just got out of their Land Rover, and there's a taxi parked behind it. I don't know the woman who just got out of it.'

Beth jumped out of bed and ran for the bathroom. 'You keep them entertained. I'm going to take a shower.'

'Make it a quick one. I don't know why they've turned up so early.' He grabbed her for a slow kiss on her way past. 'I have a feeling there'll be more explaining to do than entertaining. We have to decide how much we're going to share about our experience.'

Beth had a shower and quickly dried herself before she looked around for something more decent than track pants to pull on. There hadn't been a need for much in the way of clothing over the past few days, and most nights she and Silas had snuggled up in front of the fire together beneath a blanket, reading Alice's journals and getting to know each other more. So far, they'd learned little that they didn't already know about the travel, but Beth wasn't going to give up, hoping that Alice had somehow gone back to Branton. More journals were waiting.

She pulled on a pair of black leggings and picked up the green angora jumper from the back of the chair. A cursory brush of her hair, before she looped it up and caught it in a clip, and then dabbed on a smudge of lip gloss.

Closing the door quietly, Beth walked slowly down the stairs. The aroma of freshly-brewed coffee met her and she smiled as she walked into the parlour. David and Silas were standing by the fire; there was no sign of Megan, but she could hear low voices in the kitchen She walked over and kissed David's cheek. 'This is a nice surprise. What are you pair doing here? Where's Megan? Is everything okay?'

David pulled her in for a close hug. 'We've had a long drive overnight. It's *very* good to see you. Megan's cooking toast.'

'What happened to your famous scrambled eggs?' she asked Silas as a frisson of worry trickled in.

Silas's brow wrinkled in a frown. 'Davy wanted to talk to me. Ah. Megan's in the kitchen with—'

'With who?' she said with a quizzical glance at Silas as he looked at David. Beth headed for the kitchen, wondering who else was in there, but stopped dead and put a hand to her mouth as the door opened. Megan carried out a tray of coffee and buttered toast, but it was the woman with her who caused Beth to squeal.

'My God, Mum! What are you doing here? I was just talking about you before to Silas!'

'Hello, darling. It's lovely to see you too.' Her mother's smile seemed forced. 'I thought you were in Scotland.'

'Oh, Mum. It's great to see you.' Beth walked into her mother's open arms and hugged her. 'I was just flabbergasted when you walked out. You should have told me you were coming. I can't believe it. What are you doing here?'

'I think perhaps where you were, it may have been hard to get a message to you.' Her voice was tight. 'I'm very pleased to see you *here.*'

Beth's eyes widened as she looked from her mother to Megan, wondering how much her mother knew.

'Hello, Beth,' Megan said quietly, reaching over and squeezing Beth's hand.

'What's going on?' Beth looked around, feeling as though she had been left out of the loop again. 'Mum, have you met Silas?'

'I have. I need to have a coffee before we talk,' her mother said. 'It's a long way down here from London in a little black taxi. I was going to catch the train, but when I talked to Megan I decided to get here as fast as I could. We arrived at the same time.'

'So I see,' Beth said.

Silas must have taken pity on Beth because he walked over and took her hand. 'Be a love and pour Beth and Lucy a coffee, Megs.' He led Beth to the sofa and sat beside her and put his arm around her shoulders.

He'd made a public show of their relationship, but no one seemed terribly surprised.

'Lucy?' Beth frowned and looked around. 'Who's Lucy?'

'That's me, love.' Mum came and sat on her other side. 'My second name. Since your father and I separated, I've decided to go back to my middle name. I was always Lucy before we married. He always preferred my first name, Laura; reckoned Lucy was childish.'

'I didn't know that.' She let go of Silas's hand and opened her arms to her mother for another hug. 'It's so good to see you, Mum. Are you okay? You look . . . I don't know. You look different.'

By the time the coffee was poured, Beth was bemused; she felt as though she'd gone down the rabbit hole.

'I want to say something first before we get all serious and start talking about the travel stuff,' Megan said. 'I didn't tell you at the wedding, and then when Silas rang to say you'd disappeared, I was so upset, Beth. I worried you wouldn't get back and you'd never know. So, I want to tell you now in case you pair take off again.'

'Tell us what?' Beth frowned. 'What else has happened?'

'You're going to be a godmother. That is if you're happy to say yes.'

Beth squealed and jumped up to hug Megan. 'That is fabulous, fabulous news. The best!'

'Congratulations, Megan and David. That's wonderful,' her mother said quietly.

'Thanks, Lucy.' Megan hugged her back before she sat beside David again. 'Our lives are all changing, that's for sure.'

Beth looked curiously at her mother as she sat on the sofa. She had worked out what was different: she seemed softer and calm. Her eyes were bright, and her hands were steady. Her skin was clear and her relaxed demeanour was . . . just . . . not Mum.

Lucy? That was going to take some getting used to. Beth sat beside Silas again and his arm went around her shoulders and he held her close.

'Okay, Mum. Now tell me why you're here,' she said. 'What's going on? Are you well?'

Her mother looked at her steadily, and Beth was worried when her mother's lips trembled, and her voice shook.

'I'm well. But I came faster because I . . . I know what can happen here . . . what has happened here . . . and when I heard that you'd gone—'

'Hang on,' Beth said. 'Does the whole world know about our journey?'

'No.' Mum shook her head. 'When I arrived in London, your mobile didn't answer so I rang Megan to see if you were still in Scotland. I was hoping you were. The further you were away from this cottage the happier I would have been. I interrupted their honeymoon—'

'No, you didn't, Lucy,' David interrupted. 'I called Silas and when he told me what had happened, we headed straight back here.'

'Why, Mum? What do you know about—?'

'About the stones? The stones you went through?'

Beth's eyes widened. 'You know? I knew it!'

'Yes.' Her mother lifted her gaze and held hers steadily. 'Because I've been through them too.'

'You have? Been where? When?' Beth's mouth was open, and she shook her head. 'Why didn't you ever tell me?'

'Because I knew exactly what you would have done. You, with your love of history, and fascination with Aunt Alice. There would have been no holding you back, sweetheart.'

Beth shook her head slowly. 'I can't believe it. I want to know all about it. Did you meet Branton? Did you know if Alice got back there? I so hope she did and had a happy life. Mum, I can't believe I never knew.' She put one hand to her mouth, distressed that there was so much she hadn't known.

'No, I never met Branton, but I do know what happened. Alice told me when she came back through the last time. The year before she died. She wanted to share the knowledge of the stones, in case no one else knew before she passed away.'

Beth grabbed her mother's arm. 'What happened? Did she find him again? He was the nicest man and I know how much he loved her.'

Lucy's smile was sweet. 'She did. Alice went back, and she and Branton lived together happily as man and wife for over twenty years. Branton passed in 1523 during the English invasion of France. Sadly, he wasn't there to fight, but he was in Paris selling wool from Brue Manor. Eventually, Alice decided there was no reason to stay there—then in his time—without Branton—her grief was more bearable away from Brue Manor, and let her keep the happy memories of her life with Branton.'

David stood and came over to crouch in front of Beth and Lucy. 'You need to know. Alice travelled home and learned more about the ley lines, and her ability to traverse time more easily. She arrived back at Violet Cottage in 1968 and that's when I met her. She was a couple of years short of fifty then.'

Beth's hand went back to her mouth. 'You met Aunt Alice, David? In 1968?' It was hard to keep her voice from a screech.

'There's a few more stories you need to know, Bethie,' Megan said. 'That's when I met David too. But a little bit later. In 1971 at the Glastonbury Festival.'

Beth's head was spinning. 'My God! If I hadn't travelled myself and had Silas chase me through the stones, I'd be saying you were all mad. There's so much to take in. You *all* knew about the stones. And I never did! I can't believe it.'

Mum reached over and took Beth's hand. 'There's another story I have to tell you.'

'About Alice?'

'No, about me and your father.'

'Dad went too?'

Lucy hesitated and dropped her gaze. 'No, darling, your real father.'

'My what?'

'Your biological father. I'm going back to find him. That's why I came to England.'

Beth's world swam around her as she tried to process what Mum said. 'My *biological* father?'

Silas took her other hand and held it tightly. Whatever was coming, she had the man she loved by her side. And the man who loved her. Everything would be all right. What would Alice have said?

Time is fleeting. Seize each opportunity.

Make the most of every minute.

She swallowed and nodded. 'I'm ready, Mum. Tell me.'

'I was twenty years old, and I came over here to stay with Alice. Joshua was almost three years old.' Lucy looked past all of them to the window where the stones glowed faintly in the morning sun. 'Why I came then isn't important anymore. Why I am here now is what you need to know. I want you to know why I'm going back.'

Beth's voice shook. 'Why?'

'It's time to go back and find the man I loved and left.' Her eyes were sad as she looked at Beth. 'Your father, Bethie. The love of my life. Thomas Adams.'

Chapter One

Pilton, United Kingdom - 1851

Thomas Adams lifted one hand and wiped his damp brow as he walked along the edge of the meadow. The grass was green and lush, tempting him to remove his shoes, and let the cool grass soothe his tired feet, but the overpowering smell of cow manure was a warning that going without shoes here would not have a good outcome. He had passed some Jersey cows when he had climbed the stile where he had left his bag hidden in a clump of long grass, but now the only sign of bovine activity was the all-pervasive smell of manure. Coming from a country area, where the family pottery works were surrounded by dairies, Thomas assumed that the herd had gone to the bales for milking.

He had been directed to this unfamiliar area by one of the craftsmen at the factory, who assured him that along the edge of the dairy two miles from Pilton was a huge bank of white clay. The summer of 1851 had been hot and dry thus far, and Thomas had relished his time away from the furnaces. He had walked down from Glastonbury after leaving the train he had taken from London. He would continue his journey home to St Austell tomorrow.

While there was a plentiful supply of kaolin—the white clay used to make the white porcelain at his father's pottery works—in the valleys near the works at West Polmear on the southern coast of Cornwall, Thomas was always on the lookout for different and new resources. His father was happy to let him wander, knowing how much Thomas hated working in the heat of the furnaces. He had accepted that his youngest child was the creative son. Thomas's eldest brother oversaw the factory, while Father ran the business, and John, the middle brother, had taken over their grandparents' dairy when they had passed away.

Sourcing a new supply of kaolin would be another opportunity for them to expand. So far, Thomas had not let them down. His two-month visit to London to the Great Exhibition had been amazing and his mind was teeming with new ideas.

He rested for a moment—the walk from the train station to the farm had taken a good while, and he still had no idea of where he would spend the night, hoping that he would encounter an inn somewhere close by. If there was no inn in Pilton

Village, he would have to take the long walk back to the town of Glastonbury. A stream ran along the edge of the meadow and he stooped down and filled his hands with the sweet water, and drank deeply.

As Thomas stood, the long low moo of a cow warned him that the herd was coming back from milking, and he headed to the east, following the directions he had been given.

He strode out, keen to see this clay bank before the afternoon faded away into the dusk, seek out the owner, and then still have time to find some lodgings for the night, close enough to the station to catch the mail train back to Plymouth early tomorrow. He was not looking forward to arriving back in St Austell, because he had to face Isabelle Lyndhurst, and try to let her down gently.

Isabelle had insisted that the time he was away from her would make him realise how much he'd missed her. But truth be known, he had not given her one thought. Thomas knew that their two families were hoping for a match, but he knew that marriage would not be wise. Isabelle would think she was heartbroken, but he knew she didn't care for him as much as she desired to be the mistress of her own home. Thomas was focused on his work and was not ready to give his heart to a woman—especially a whining, clinging woman—no matter how persuasive she was.

Ahead was the forest that he had been told edged the unusual bank of clay, but the closer he walked to the trees, the more he wondered whether the directions he had been given had been accurate. The land was flattening out and there was no sign of any hills ahead.

Thomas stopped and put one hand to his eyes, turning in a complete arc as he examined the landscape around him. He blinked as a shaft of noon sunlight hit a tall rock ahead of him, and bright light bathed the Jersey herd in an eerie blue glow. He blinked again and stared at the rocks, but the glow disappeared and his gaze was met only by the soft afternoon sunlight. Excitement built as a glimpse of white caught his attention and he hurried towards the rocks. Was it the bank of clay he was looking for?

Setting off in that direction, he paused and frowned, taking care where he walked. There must be beehives on the other side of the three rocks ahead. A low and constant hum broke the silence.

He blinked as a white shape moved ahead of him.

Chapter Two

Sydney - February, 2019

Time is fleeting. Seize each opportunity. Make the most of every minute.

Lucy McLaren closed her eyes as thoughts of the past swirled through her head. She'd hoped that the noise of the wine bar where she was meeting her best friend, Mel, would cocoon her from her thoughts, but there was no such luck. Laura had gone back to her preferred name of Lucy after Royden had left.

When Joshua and Beth had been born, Royden had agreed to compromise; Joshua had taken his father's surname, but Laura had stood her ground and Beth had retained the family name of McLaren when she was born four years after Joshua.

'The women of our family have always taken the family name,' she'd insisted. It was the first time she had ever stood up to Royden, and knowing what she knew then, made it easy for Lucy to be strong. Staying with Royden Fitzgerald had been a huge mistake. A mistake that she was reminded of many times in the almost thirty years they were together. Her strength to stay came from the life-changing experience the year before Beth was born. The secret she had carried with her for more than half her life had only been shared with one other person—her Aunt Alice.

Only guilt had kept Laura in Sydney, despite Alice's pleas that she leave Royden.

'I don't like the man. He saps your light,' Alice said when Lucy and Royden took the children for a visit to the cottage when Beth was nine, and Joshua was about to start high school. They'd visited Euro Disney and then gone on to visit Alice in Somerset. 'He is cruel to you, and both you and the children would be better off without him.'

'You and I both know there is no alternative, Alice. We can't all be free like you.' Lucy felt guilty now remembering how disparaging she'd been then of Alice's hippie lifestyle.

'Don't be so hasty to jump to that conclusion,' her aunt had said. 'Look at my life. I found the courage to go back and I had many happy years with Branton.'

'But I have the children to consider here and *now*.' Lucy sighed. 'I will stay. Perhaps I'll think about it when they both grow up.'

'Lucy? You know what I say, don't you.' Alice flicked her braid over her shoulder impatiently.

'I do. *Time is fleeting. Seize each opportunity. Make the most of every minute.*' Lucy folded her arms. 'But Alice, I have commitments and I have children who must be provided for.'

'I know, darling. But can I ask you one thing? Promise me you will try one day.'

'I promise,' Lucy had said quietly.

Alice passed on ten years later, and they went back to Somerset to sort the cottage. But it had taken another ten years after Joshua and Beth had left home for Lucy to begin to find herself, and finally decide to seize the opportunity and seek out the past. When Royden had finally left her for his secretary last year it had been a huge relief. Her guilt no longer kept her there.

Lucy glanced at her watch, and then took another sip of the crisp, cold Chardonnay. When she'd told Mel she had some news, her friend had insisted on meeting at the wine bar. Lucy was wary; she knew she'd drunk too much for a few months when Royden had first left, so tonight was a one-wine chat, and then she'd move to soda water.

Even though she'd been happy that their relationship was finally over; the thought of Royden taking up with a woman younger than Beth had been a blow to Lucy's almost fifty-year-old self-esteem.

'Darling.' She looked up as Mel slipped onto the stool beside her and reached over to kiss both Lucy's cheeks. 'Sorry I'm late. I got caught up in the office. Another Chardy for you, or shall we get a bottle of bubbles?'

'No. This is it for me, thanks, Mel. I'm driving home.'

'Aw, come on Laur—I mean Lucy.' Her friend put her bag on the other stool. 'I still can't get used to Lucy! You've been very circumspect, and very forgiving of Royden. I would have strung him up by the—'

'It was tempting,' Lucy chuckled. 'But he's done me a favour. You know I've never been happy. And I've always been Lucy to *me*.'

Mel came back with a bottle of champagne and two glasses.

Lucy pulled a face at her. 'Just one and then you can take the rest home with you.'

Mel grinned at her. 'I know if you have a couple of drinks, you'll tell me more about what's happening, darling. I have no idea why you stayed with Royden for so long. He's not a nice man, Lucy. He isolated you and kept you from your friends, and the few times we did come to your place, he made us feel so unwelcome, no one wanted to come back.'

'I know. But there was a lot more than you knew, Mel. I only ever planned to stay until the kids grew up.'

'So tell me why you stayed for so much longer. I know he doesn't give two hoots about your kids. How long since they've seen him?'

Lucy shrugged. 'Beth's wiped him, and Joshua's been in the north for a couple of years now. I don't think they're in touch. Josh doesn't say much. I'm flying up to see him before I leave.'

'Leave? Leave for where?'

'I'm flying to London from Cairns after I see Josh. Beth went over for Megan's wedding and after she tours Scotland, she's staying in my aunt's cottage in Somerset. I want to see her. And then I have a journey of my own to make.' Lucy reached out and took Mel's hand. 'You've been a long and loyal friend, love. And I wish I could tell you where I was going but you'd think I was crazy. I'll get Beth to keep in touch with you, and let you know when I leave. There's no internet, email, or phone where I'm going.'

'I didn't think there was anywhere like that in the world these days.' Mel shook her head. 'You'll have to write a snail mail to me. Don't lose touch.'

'No post either.'

'Bloody hell, woman. Where are you going? Siberia?'

Lucy chuckled and accepted the glass of bubbles Mel held out. 'You're such a city gal, Mel.'

'Okay, I might be, but I'm happy.' Mel clinked her glass against Lucy's. 'So here's to new beginnings and a happy future for my best friend.'

Lucy nodded and reached up and touched the tiny white porcelain ornaments on the fine gold chain she always wore around her neck. 'I like the sound of that. And let's toast a happier past too.'

Mel looked at her curiously. 'How many wines have you had? Sorry, love, the past stays as it was.'

Lucy smiled as she thought of her happier past. If she could recapture it, she would not be coming home.

Chapter Three

Pilton, United Kingdom - 1851

Thomas walked across the field, but there was no sign of any bees, and now the humming had stopped. He kept one eye on the large bull grazing under the spreading oak tree on the other side of the rock where he was sure he'd seen a flash of white. For a moment he'd thought it was a person. He frowned as he got closer; it couldn't be the clay as the land was flat and covered with green grass. The white must have been a flash of sunlight as the sun climbed to its zenith. It was very warm, and Thomas blinked as the scene ahead wavered. His throat was parched, but he'd check around the other side of the rocks before he went back to the stream. It would be just his luck not to go far enough and miss the clay. Maybe it wasn't a bank? Maybe it was a seam of white clay in the middle of the field? He'd seen that up in Devonshire last time he'd gone to the factories in Staffordshire. After he'd had another drink he'd head to Glastonbury and find some lodgings for the night.

It appeared to have been a wasted trip. He should have stayed on the train; he would have almost been back to St Austell by now. There was plenty of work awaiting him at the factory, and he was keen to implement some of the innovations he'd seen in London.

The Great Exhibition at Crystal Palace had exceeded his wildest expectations. Even the structure that held the myriad of displays had been amazing. Architecturally adventurous, the building was almost two thousand feet long, constructed entirely of glass on a cast-iron frame. Opulent fabrics from every corner of the world, flax, silks and linens surrounded them. General hardware, brass and ironwork of many types, locks, grates. Innovative machines and implements, marine engines, hydraulic presses, and machinery in motion—the scope of the display was incredible. But Thomas had made his way to the displays of porcelain from all over Europe. Delft from Holland, Sevres from France, as well as different porcelain pieces from Austria, Switzerland, Italy and Germany. He had spent two days talking to the designer from Meissen; the days where attempts had been made to stop *arcanum*–the secrets of porcelain production—spreading across Europe had long gone, and now the designers and factory owners were proudly displaying their wares at this world exhibition.

'Two types of porcelain are made in our factory, the high-fired hard-paste porcelain,' the German had told him in impeccable English.

'Ours is the variety first made in China using kaolin,' Thomas had replied. 'We have been experimenting with that in St Austell. As well as the low-fired soft-paste porcelain.' He had found it hard to leave London but knew that his father would be anxious for his return to the Cornwall factory.

The new varieties of white porcelain on display had intrigued him, and he knew he could create some new designs that exceeded the quality of those that he'd seen. He was keen to get home and share his ideas with the team of designers. Perhaps he wouldn't have to go back to the furnaces at all. If only he could source a new site for the unique white clay needed.

He looked ahead and the spires of Glastonbury shimmered in the bright wavering light. Another shimmer of white moved ahead and Thomas quickened his pace. As he reached the three strangely-shaped rocks, he held back a cry of surprise as a woman, dressed in white, stepped from behind the centre rock. Her eyes were wide and as she stared at him, she held out one hand to him before crumpling gracefully to the ground.

'Mistress?' Thomas dropped to the ground beside her, unsure of what do to. She was a young woman with brown hair and flawless skin, but her lips were bloodless. 'Can you hear me?' Without thinking, he tore his shirt off, rolled it into a ball and placed it beneath her head, checking that she hadn't hit her head as she'd fallen, but there appeared to be no rocks on the grass. Only the three large shapes loomed above them.

He lifted her hand and it was cold to the touch. As he leaned over, her eyelids flickered, and then as she looked at his bare chest, her eyes widened.

'It is all right, Mistress. I removed my shirt to put it beneath your head. I mean you no harm.'

'Where am I? What happened?' She lifted a shaking hand to her head. 'My head hurts and my eyes are blurry. Do I know you? I can barely see you.'

Thomas frowned. Her accent was strange, such as he'd never heard before; even though they had workers from all over Europe in their factory, he didn't recognise the accent.

'No, you do not know me. I think you fell. Come, I will take you to the stream and sit you down in the shade.'

'Wait? Where's Joshua?' As she looked around, a distressed cry broke from her lips. 'Where's my baby?'

Chapter Four

Cairns, Australia, March - 2019

'Mum, it's so good to see you.' Joshua, her eldest child took Lucy's carry-on bag as he greeted her in the arrivals hall of Cairns airport. 'But a surprise. I was really pleased to get your text last night. A holiday?'

Lucy slipped her arm through Joshua's as they walked across to the baggage carousel. 'No, a long journey. I wanted to see you before I leave.'

'Leave?' He frowned. 'Where are you going?'

'I'm going to the UK to stay in Aunt Alice's cottage, and I'm not sure when I'll be back.' Lucy swallowed. Saying goodbye to Mel had been hard because she knew there was a good chance she wouldn't come back. Saying goodbye to Joshua was going to be a lot harder. 'You remember the cottage in Somerset? We went there before you started high school. When we went to Paris to Euro Disney.'

'I do. Dad hated being there. It was a pretty tense time. I remember our other visit too.'

Lucy stared at her son. 'Our other visit?'

'Yes, when I was just a little tacker. Before Beth was born.'

Lucy opened her eyes in disbelief. 'No way! Do you remember that visit? You wouldn't even have been three when we were over there.'

'I do. When you went away, Aunty Alice gave me a birthday party on the village green. All I can remember was the homemade ice cream, and she had a thing with ribbons on it that we all held as we ran around a post. All the village children came.' He grinned. 'I ate too much ice cream and I spewed on the grass.'

'My goodness.' Lucy put a hand on her chest. 'I can't believe you remember. All that detail.'

'I do remember you were gone a long time and when I cried at night, Aunty Alice would take me for a walk to make me tired enough to sleep. Where did you go? Were you working? Dad didn't go on that trip, did he?'

The baggage carousel kicked into life, and Lucy had time to think about her answer.

'No, we went by ourselves. There's my bag, Josh. The olive-green one with the yellow ribbon on the handle. I'll tell you all about my trip when we get to the hotel. I've booked into the Sheraton.'

'Dinner tonight?'

'Sounds good.'

'There's someone I'd like you to meet. Could I bring a . . . a friend?'

Lucy raised her eyebrows. 'Sounds interesting. I'll look forward to it.'

Joshua dropped her at the hotel, and headed back to the city radio station where he presented the breakfast show. Sometimes when Lucy missed her kids, she'd stream his show over the internet just to hear her son's voice. There'd be none of that where she was going. She unpacked her PJs and a dress to wear to dinner that would double up for the long haul flight tomorrow, and then she ran a bubble bath in the luxurious marble bathroom.

Slipping into the scented water, Lucy put her head back and wondered how much she'd tell Joshua. It was only fair to tell him the truth; she suspected that Beth would have discovered the secrets of the cottage if she had been reading Alice's diaries and journals. Joshua would probably think she was crazy, and she still wasn't sure if she would tell him or not.

The problem was, could she tell her son the truth without losing his respect?

##

'Mum, this is Amanda. Amanda, my mum, Laura.'

'Lucy, these days, Josh,' she interrupted. 'Since your Dad and I split I go by the name I prefer now. The name I always had before we were married.'

Joshua shot her a quizzical look. 'Okay, Amanda, meet my mum . . . Lucy.'

The pretty dark-haired girl reached out and took Lucy's hand. 'It's lovely to finally meet you, Lucy. I've heard a lot about you.'

'That sounds serious.' Lucy looked at Joshua.

'Amanda and I have moved in together, Mum. She's been nagging me to take her down to Sydney so she could meet you.' He pulled a face. 'But you know me, I'm slack and I take time to get around to things.'

The subtext was there; Joshua stayed away from Sydney because he didn't want to see his father. For a while, when she and Royden had finally split, she had worried that she'd fallen into the same avoidance category for Joshua as his father did.

'But I promise I *was* going to come and see you before we set the wedding date.' His smile was wide, and Lucy hugged them both.

'That's wonderful news. Have you told Beth yet?'

'No. I haven't been able to get onto her. I only proposed last week.'

Amanda held out her left hand and Lucy admired the lovely diamond and sapphire ring.

'Probably no phone service in the castle where the wedding is,' she said.

'I was going to suggest she flew back to Sydney via Cairns and we could spend some time together,' Joshua added.

'Well, I won't let on when I catch up with her. I'll let you tell her your news.'

The conversation over dinner was lively, Lucy and Joshua caught her up with all their news, and Lucy learned a lot more about Amanda and her work as a primary school teacher. The more she watched her with Joshua, the happier she could see her son was. As they waited for their coffee, Lucy turned to the young girl and took her hand. 'I'm really happy for you. I'm pleased Joshua has you. It makes it easier for me to go away, knowing he has a partner.'

'You still haven't told us about your trip, Mum.'

Lucy folded her napkin and put it on the table. 'Yes. Um. No. I haven't, have I?'

Joshua frowned. 'Is there a problem? Is there something you don't want me—us—to know?'

Lucy sat straight and still. 'I'm going away for a long time, and there's a chance I may not come back.'

'You're going to move to the UK?'
'Possibly.'

'I'm not getting it, Mum. You haven't decided yet?'

'Not one hundred percent.'

Joshua's mouth set in a straight line. 'Is Dad still giving you a hard time?'

'He was for a while if I let him, yes, but I have very little—if anything—to do with him now.'

'Fair enough. Well, when you know what you're doing, let us know. If you move there, we can come and visit. Amanda was talking about a European honeymoon, weren't you, love?'

Amanda nodded and smiled at Lucy. 'We were, and it would be lovely to visit you.'

'Will you be travelling around or staying at Aunt Alice's place?' Joshua asked.

'I'll base myself there,' Lucy said carefully, 'but I do intend taking a big trip. And when I'm travelling I won't be able to be contacted.'

A frown wrinkled Joshua's forehead. 'You make me feel guilty, Mum. I should have come down to see if you were all right.'

Lucy reached out and took both his hands. 'I'm fine, darling. You have your own life to live now, and it makes me happy to see you happy. If things work out like I'm hoping, I'll be in a happy place too.' She cleared her throat and spoke briskly before emotion took over. She had come to a snap decision; she couldn't tell Joshua the truth. Not yet.

'Now, if you're finished your coffees, I'm going to say goodnight and goodbye'—her voice trembled—'because I won't see you tomorrow. My flight leaves while you're on-air in the morning.'

'I can get my stand-in, to do my shift, Mum.'

'No, Josh.' Lucy shook her head. 'We'll say our goodbyes now.'

As they stood outside the restaurant waiting for their taxis, Joshua wrapped his arms around Lucy. 'You take care of yourself, Mum, and we'll come and see you. Wherever you are when we come over, we'll find out and come and visit, even if it's in the wilds of Scotland.'

Lucy blinked away tears. 'That would be wonderful.' She turned and hugged Amanda and then reached up and pressed her lips against her son's cheek.

'Whatever happens, just remember I love you, Josh.'

'And I love you too, Mum.' Her son held her close until the taxi pulled up. With one last anguished look at her eldest child, Lucy ran for the taxi and didn't look back as it pulled away from the kerb. That time many years ago when she had lost her son for a whole month filled her mind. Those weeks had been hard, but taking the step she intended to take soon, would mean that she may lose both her children forever.

Could she do it?

Would the happiness of going back, make up for perhaps never seeing her two children again?

Chapter Five

Pilton, United Kingdom - 1851

Lucy McLaren blinked and put her hand to her cheek where cool water was trickling down from a damp cloth. The tall man standing above her had pressed his handkerchief against the swelling on her forehead after he had dipped it in a stream close by. She had handed his shirt back when she had sat up, and he'd turned away while he had put it back on.

'Thank you,' she said. 'I feel better now. I'm not sure what happened.'

''Tis a very warm day,' he said. 'Unseasonably so. You must have a touch of heatstroke.'

Lucy shook her head. 'This isn't hot. Not for an Aussie.'

He frowned but didn't say anything.

'I'll walk back to my aunt's cottage. It's not very far. My little boy will be there with her. I'm sorry I panicked before.'

'I'll accompany you.' His language was stilted and formal, but Lucy was grateful for him helping her.

'It's cool,' she said. 'It's only over there past the—'

Her head spun again as she stared over to the lane where the cottages were.

'Past the gate, I was going to say. Oh, I must be lost. I didn't think I'd come so far. I can't see the fence or the gate. Or the lane.'

'Let's head back that way together,' he said.

For the first time, Lucy looked at the guy who'd been sitting beside her when she'd become aware of her surroundings. His skin was fair but it was his deep blue eyes and jet black eyelashes that held her attention. His hair was dark, but his lashes were so dark they could have been tinted. Her eyes lowered and she hesitated as she looked at the way he was dressed. When he'd stood and hurried across to the field, she had seen he was tall and broad. Dressed in old-fashioned clothes, his creased shirt looked to be linen. It was crumpled from being rolled up and beneath her head.

'Are you on the way to a party?' she asked. 'I don't want to take up your time. I'll be fine. Like I said, it's cool.'

He looked at her strangely. 'It's actually quite warm.'

'No, I mean cool, you know, as in sweet.'

His dark brows came together. 'Mistress, you seem to have some confusion with your words. You appear to have a head injury. Come, I'll take you to your home.'

Mistress? Looked like she'd been rescued by the village eccentric.

'What time is it?' Lucy looked down at her digital watch, but the screen was blank. As she looked closer, she noticed a fine crack across the glass. 'Oh no, I must have broken my watch when I fell.'

'I have never seen a fob watch worn like that before.' He looked at her wrist curiously. 'And the hands have fallen off the clockface.'

'No, it's a digital watch. Look, I've got to hurry. My little boy will be ready for his tea, and I don't want to leave him with my aunt for too long. He's too energetic for her sometimes. And she has a bad habit of leaving him in the bath by himself. I mean, I know he's almost three, but I still prefer to watch him.' Lucy turned around, trying to figure out which way to go. There was no signpost at the end of the lane. 'Do you know my Aunt? Alice McLaren?'

'No, I'm sorry, I don't. I'm not from around here. I was looking for some clay in the field when I saw you fall. Now, come. When I get you safely home I must seek lodging for the night. Tomorrow, I shall take the train back to Cornwall.'

'Seek lodging?' Lucy parroted, her tone disbelieving. *Who was this guy?*

'Yes, I believe there is an inn or two in Glastonbury. Unless there is one in Pilton, but I haven't reached that village yet.'

Lucy took a step back, feeling a bit unsafe for the first time. She wasn't going anywhere with this dude. 'All good. You go to town and I'll head home. Thanks for looking after me, anyway. I'm fine now.'

He hesitated, and she held his gaze and felt reassured. His eyes were kind, and he looked harmless enough, despite his strange words and clothes.

'Very well, if you are sure. But I will watch you from here. If that is all right with you.'

'Thank you.' Lucy held out her hand to shake his. 'I appreciate it. By the way, I'm Lucy McLaren. Good luck with finding a room.'

He nodded and took her hand. ''Tis a pleasure, albeit a strange one, to meet you, Lucy. I am Thomas Adams, but I'm mostly known as young Tom.'

'Well, young Tom, thanks again. See you around, maybe, one day.'

'Around?'

Lucy shrugged. 'I might see you in town if you ever come back this way.'

'Oh, yes, I may well do. Very well. You go and I shall watch until you are safely there.'

Lucy strode off across the field in the direction she thought the cottage was, very much aware of the eyes of the strange man watching her every step.

Chapter Six

London, March - 2019

Lucy wondered if she being extremely foolish as the jet winged its way to London. Maybe she should just forget this obsession of rediscovering her past. Maybe it was a midlife crisis, although if she was honest, she had never forgotten the man she hoped to find. Or stopped loving him. Her fingers went to the necklace at her throat.

She knew she had been lucky to have had a love like that, no matter how fleeting it had been. The memory and the dreams had kept her going through the difficult times in her life, and every time she'd looked at Beth she remembered the man she loved.

'Thank you.' Lucy took the cup of water the steward offered and settled back in her seat. Maybe she could get some sleep and stop overthinking.

She had come this far; she would continue with her plan. It all depended on Beth, and how she was. Knowing her daughter had been living in Alice's cottage made her nervous. Beth took after Lucy; if she got an idea in her head, she was tenacious, and she'd follow it through. Lucy vowed to call her as soon as they landed, and then she would catch a train down to Somerset. Excitement squirmed in her stomach as she thought of being in Somerset again.

Her life there seemed like a dream now—the first visit anyway, when she and Joshua had fled from Sydney when she'd discovered Royden's first affair.

The second visit, when she and Royden had taken both the children to see Alice, had been one of the most stressful periods in Lucy's life. Being so close, yet so far away, had been intolerable. When they had gone over the last time with Beth a few years ago it had been a last-ditch attempt to save her relationship with Royden. Lucy had reasoned if she could go over and forget the past while she was there in Somerset where she had met Tom, they might have a chance. The email she'd seen Royden reading on his phone on the way home had woken her up for good. It was from the same woman he'd been seeing for the past three years. Their life together was over; if she was honest it had been for a long time. She'd often wondered if she hadn't fallen pregnant with Joshua, how long she would have stayed with him. Spending a lifetime with a man she'd never loved, and lately had no respect for, was hard, and such a waste; Lucy vowed to herself that what was left of her life would be spent in a better way. Even if she was alone if things didn't work out as she hoped they would.

Even though Royden had told her the early affair, which had resulted in her fleeing to Somerset thirty years ago, had been his first, and he'd promised her it would never happen again, there had been many other lapses over the years, and the foolish guilt Lucy carried had led to her forgiveness each time.

She too had erred, so how could she take Royden to task for the same thing?

But as the years passed, Lucy knew she couldn't believe a word that came out of Royden's mouth. She sometimes wondered why he stayed because he wasn't a good father nor was he particularly interested in either of the children. Lucy had been the mother who went to school functions and Saturday sport and listened to the teenage woes as Joshua and Beth began to make their own way in life. She hadn't been surprised when they had both left home as soon as they left school.

Lucy put her head back and closed her eyes. Fancy Joshua remembering that first trip. An image came into her mind, and she smiled and slipped into sleep.

##

The trip to London seemed to take forever, and when she disembarked Lucy hurried across to the baggage carousel. Unease niggled when Beth's phone went straight to voicemail again. She'd tried as soon as they'd landed, and then after she'd freshened up in the restrooms. As she stood waiting for her luggage, she tried again, but with the same result—straight to voicemail.

Maybe Beth was still in Scotland and out of service. But the wedding had been ten days ago; she thought she'd be back at the cottage by now.

Lucy stood there chewing her lip and came to a decision. She pressed the speed dial for Megan, feeling a little guilty because Megan and David were still on their honeymoon.

'Hi, Lucy.' Megan sounded surprised that she had called.

'Hello, Megan, I'm so sorry to bother you. I know you're on your honeymoon, but I wondered if you've heard from Beth lately?'

'No, not since they left here,' Megan said. 'How long since you've talked to her?'

They?

'Not since before the wedding. I've tried to call a few times, but I can't get through. I'm at Heathrow and I'm going down to the cottage. And who is "they"?'

'Um, Silas is one of David's friends. He was driving Beth back and staying in David's cottage next door.'

'Oh, that's good. I needn't worry.'

'I'll get David to give Silas a call and see if he can get on to him. I'll call you back.'

'Thank you, Megan. I apologise again for bothering you.'

'No, not at all. I hope we can catch up while you're here. I'm sure we'll head down to Somerset soon. David and Silas write songs together, and he was talking about a visit in the not too distant future.'

'I'll stay at the cottage for a short while if it suits Beth, so hopefully, we can catch up.'

'Okay, bye for now, Lucy. I'll text you as soon as we hear back from Silas.'

'Thank you. I appreciate it. I know I'm a worry wart, but that's a mother thing.'

Lucy collected her luggage and headed for the train that would take her to Paddington station.

Chapter Seven

Pilton, United Kingdom - 1851

Thomas waited in the shade and watched as the beautiful young woman walked purposefully across the field. It appeared she knew where she was going.

For a few moments, he wondered if she was sunstruck, but she had seemed to gather her wits about her as she spoke in that strange accent, and using words he had never heard before. He watched as she walked across the field, in the direction away from the town ahead, and then he turned away, as he realised he must go and find himself a bed and a meal for the night.

The story of the white clay appeared to be just that—a story—and he wondered whether he should look further in the morning. With a frown he tried to remember what he had been told, and as he recalled the conversation he realised that he had seen no dairy in the local vicinity. There had been cattle, but no dairy where he had been walking.

The craftsman had said the clay bank was at the edge of the dairy two miles from Pilton. Perhaps he had come too far to the east. Thomas nodded. He would seek a bed, and rise early on the morrow, and then look in the other direction.

Yes, that would be his plan. He was very keen to find this clay—if indeed it existed—as the exhibition had filled him with so many new ideas. He was torn between wasting time searching for the clay or hurrying back to the factory to put his new ideas into a design.

Perhaps later tonight after he had eaten, he would take out his sketch pad and add to the designs he had drawn as he had taken the train down from London.

He turned and began to walk towards the township of Glastonbury, where he was sure to find lodgings. Thomas chastised himself. He had not planned this trip at all well. The Arthurian legend had always fascinated him, and he regretted not leaving himself more time to explore the district; he had been too focused on finding the clay and getting back to St Austell to work.

He paused and looked ahead at the magical spire gracing the top of Glastonbury Tor. The sky was a pale blue with threads of white cloud, and the air was still as the afternoon approached.

Thomas drew a deep breath and decided that if he could get lodgings for two or three days, he would stay longer. Perhaps he may also encounter the woman who had told him her name was Lucy.

As he came to the decision, he began to walk.

A loud and distressed cry stopped him in his tracks. He turned back towards the rocks where Lucy had appeared and was taken aback to see her running towards him.

As she got closer he could see the distress on her face. She reached him and grabbed at his arms. Her hair was in disarray and her blouse was hanging loose over a pair of wide trousers such as he had never seen a woman wear before. He had been too taken with her before to notice that she was wearing men's clothing. He had assumed she was wearing a long skirt.

'Lucy? What is it? What's happened?'

'They're gone. They're not there. My baby has gone.' Her sobs were ragged, and she drew a deep breath.

'Gone? Who are they?'

'My aunt and my . . . my baby. They're gone.' Her eyes were wide and her words came in a pant. 'I'm sure I went to our cottage. It was in the same spot, but it looked different. I tried to open the door, but a strange woman came outside and asked what I wanted.'

He held her hand gently as she stared up at him, her eyes full of distress. 'I am sure they have not gone. Perhaps you are a little disoriented from hitting your head.'

'No. I told her I was looking for the cottage of my aunt, Alice McLaren. She stared at me and said it was the McLaren cottage but there was no Alice there.'

'It must be a different cottage.'

'No.' Her voice was fierce. 'The lane is the right one and the fields are the same and the large tree is still between the stones and the fence—' Her words broke off, and her mouth dropped open and a look of absolute horror crossed her face.

'What is it?'

Her hands were suddenly cold in his. 'My God. No. It can't be.'

'Speak slowly. It can't be what?'

Her agitation was increasing by the second and Thomas wondered how he could help her. How he could calm this beautiful, yet strange, woman.

'The stones,' she said in a whisper so low he had to incline his head to hear her words. She stepped back and looked at him intently. 'If it is the stones like Alice told me,'—she shook her head and laughed, but her laugh held no mirth—'it will explain why Alice and Joshua aren't there.' Her breath hitched and her panic began to rise. 'I'm not there. Oh my God, Joshua.'

'Please, Lucy. Come with me. I am going to see if we can take you to a doctor. You are going to make yourself ill again.'

She pulled away. 'I'm not ill, and I'm not imagining this.' Her pretty eyes narrowed as she pulled away from his hands. 'Tell me quickly, what is the date. What day is it? What year is it?' Her voice began to rise in pitch again, and Thomas was bewildered. He had never encountered such strange behaviour before, and he knew he could not leave her yet.

'It is the first day of July. And that explains why it is so unseasonably warm.' The more he thought about her behaviour, the more he believed she had taken too much sun.

'I will take you into the town, and we will cool you down, and make sure you are well. Then I will take you home to your cottage. We will find the right one, please don't worry.'

Her hands held his arm tightly, and her words were clipped. 'What year is it?'

'Year?' he repeated.

'Yes, what year is it? What is the year? Please, Tom, tell me. What is the year?'

'It is 1851. The year of the Great Exhibition in London, which is where I have been for the past two months.'

'1851? I knew it!' She took a step away from him, and before he could move, her eyes rolled backwards and she fell into his arms in another faint.

As he held her, Thomas tried to make sense of what she was saying.

Why did Lucy want to know the year? And what was it that she said she knew? Whatever it was, was distressing enough to make her faint again. Perhaps she was ill.

He tried to rouse her by tapping gently on her cheek, but she sighed and turned her head away without opening her eyes.

What could he do? He couldn't leave her here by herself in the state she was in? Nor could he make her walk into Glastonbury with him.

There was only one thing for it; he was going to have to carry her. And he would have to retrieve his bag on the way.

Chapter Eight

Glastonbury, 1851

Lucy was aware of being carried, but the certainty that she had gone through Aunt Alice's stones firmed with each step the man called Thomas took. She kept her eyes closed as she desperately tried to remember what had happened. She and Joshua had been walking in the field looking at the black and white cows. Joshua had run ahead and she had chased him and stumbled as she passed the three tall stones. The next thing she knew was waking up with an aching head, lying on the cool grass, and to her distress, for the first few minutes, she hadn't even remembered that Joshua had been with her.

Please God, that Aunt Alice had seen them from the cottage and come to get Joshua. Aunt Alice had been up in her bedroom when they left and there was a fine view of the fields and the stones from the top floor of the cottage. Lucy drew in a breath and moaned as she thought of the stream that edged the meadow. Joshua was fascinated with floating little bark boats in the water.

Please, oh please, let him be safe. He was such a little boy.

'Are you awake, Lucy?' She kept her eyes closed and shook her head slightly.

'Lucy?'

Slowly her eyes opened and she looked up into the face of the man who held her in his arms.

'I am taking you into the town, and I will get a room for you until we sort out what is happening. I will see if there is a doctor there to check that you are in good health.'

'My health is fine,' she snapped. 'It is my present situation that is the problem.'

'I shall help you with that, but first, we must get to the town and seek lodging for the night.' He looked down at her and the expression in his eyes reassured her. 'Tomorrow we will go back to your cottage and see what they have to say.'

As she looked up at him, Lucy decided she could trust Tom. He was kind, and he seemed sincere; he had no reason to lie, and no reason to help a strange woman he had encountered in a field.

Lucy looked down at her clothes as she tried to accept what had happened.

What she thought had happened.

Her white cheesecloth trousers and her embroidered shirt would look strange to him if her suspicions were correct. No wonder he had looked at her like that when she had noticed her watch was broken. Did they have watches here? Now? She doubted it.

She shook her head slightly and tried not to let fear take hold as she realised what had happened to her. She had stumbled at the stones that Aunt Alice had told her about, and she had left Joshua back in her time and somehow had ended up in—when had he said?

1851?

A sob hitched her breath.

She had listened to Alice's stories and had accepted them, but she had never in a million years been tempted to try it for herself.

'Hush, it's all right. I will look after you.'

***

The beautiful young woman—Lucy, she had called herself—was light in Tom's arms as he carried her across the fields. From her skin came a strange, but pleasant, perfume. A fragrance that was unfamiliar to him.

Her sob had unsettled him, and he tried to console her. To his surprise, his thoughts of finding the clay bank, and his intent to get his design ideas onto paper, had fled, and his focus was entirely on the young woman he carried in his arms. She was slight, but he stopped and rested when he retrieved his bag.

Tom wanted to help her. Her story was strange, but although he didn't understand why he believed her; he did not think that she had come from an asylum or that she was lying to him for her own purposes. For a fleeting moment, he had wondered if she belonged to the gypsies he had seen in the field a mile or so from the railway station in their horse-drawn wagon, but had soon dismissed that thought as her skin was fair. She fascinated him, and the desire to help her was overwhelming. It was as though he couldn't let her out of his sight.

Tom forced his gaze away from her face as they made their way. Over two hours had passed and they rested occasionally. In the distance, in the gathering dusk, he could see the spires of the township.

''Tis not far now, Mistress Lucy. We shall find somewhere to stay and eat shortly.'

She nodded and tried to lift herself in his arms. 'I'm okay to walk now.'

'Okay?' He frowned, not sure what she meant.

'I am fine to walk. Please put me down.'

Tom stopped walking and she slid from his arms to her feet. The soft material of her clothing brushed against his arms. It was as soft as silk but thicker, and more like the linen of his shirt, but still with a softness.

'Put your arm through mine, in case you feel faint again,' he said.

She hesitated for a moment and then her hand slipped through the crook of his arm. 'Thank you, Tom.'

They walked quietly along the road, and soon they began to pass people strolling in the early evening. Occasionally heads would turn as the women looked at Lucy's strange apparel.

Tom paused as they passed a middle-aged couple, with a pleasant demeanour.

'Excuse me, sir?'

The gentleman stopped walking and nodded at Tom. 'Yes, young man? How can I help you?'

'My . . . er . . . sister and I are arriving late to your town and are seeking a respectable lodging house for the night. Are you able to set us in the direction of such an establishment?'

'Of course. There is the George Hotel on the High Street. You cannot miss it. It stands out not only because of its age. It is an imposing edifice, three-storied with mullion windows and panelled stone facing the street.'

'It is a very respectable establishment,' the woman holding the man's arm added. 'Above the arched front door, you will see three carved panels bearing the coats of arms of Glastonbury Abbey and King Edward IV.'

Tom nodded. 'Is the High Street far from here?' He looked ahead as several streets branched off the road they were following.

'The third street to your left, young sir.'

'And then along about two hundred yards,' the woman added. 'You will also find a hearty meal there.'

Tom nodded. 'Thank you, and have a good evening.'

As they left the older couple, Lucy grabbed his arm and held it tightly. 'I can't stay in the town. I don't have my purse with me, and even if I did, I wouldn't have the right money.'

'Don't worry yourself. I can take care of that. I will get you a room, we will eat, and once the morning comes, I will take you back to your cottage and we will find out what we can.'

'Thank you.'

Tom was surprised when Lucy's fingers kept a tight hold on his arm.

Chapter Nine

Glastonbury, 1851

Lucy woke with a start. She rolled over, her eyes opening quickly as she felt for Joshua lying beside her, but the bed was empty. They had shared a bed in the spare bedroom in Aunt Alice's cottage since they had arrived two weeks ago. She hadn't talked to Royden yet, even though he had rung the cottage several times; the anger that had consumed her was still too fresh. His betrayal when they had been together for such a short time, and their son was only—almost—three years old, had cut her to the quick.

Her breath came in a gasp as the events of the day before came slamming back, and she bit back an anguished cry. She had to know that Joshua was safe. He had to be with Aunt Alice; she couldn't bear to think of him wandering alone in the fields, looking for her, lost and crying.

She put her hands over her face. Joshua was a smart little boy; when he hadn't been able to find her he would have turned around and gone back to the cottage.

Alice would know what had happened. She had talked to Lucy of her journeys and told her that it seemed to be the McClaren women who could go through the stones with little trouble. Lucy had only half-believed her, and they had been going to speak of it more that night when Joshua had gone to sleep.

If only they had finished the conversation, and she knew what to do now. There must be a way to get back; there had to be. Alice had travelled back and forth on many occasions, she had told Lucy.

As she swung her legs to the patterned rug on the floor, there was a soft tap on the door.

'Lucy? Are you awake?'

Tom had brought her to this hotel last night, ensured she had eaten and then had secured two rooms, one for himself and one for her, who he had referred to as "his sister". He had been kind and considerate, and an absolute gentleman. He had tried to distract her from her worry about Joshua as they had eaten bowls of thick vegetable soup in the small dining room at the back of the lower floor of the hotel.

'I am still in awe of the merchandise that I saw at the exhibition,' he said as they ate, his eyes wide. Thomas was a good-looking man; his dark eyes and olive skin gave him an exotic appearance and for a few minutes Lucy put her worry aside and listened to him as he told her what he had seen.

'Porcelain figures, of the purest white,' he said. 'And fine ornaments that looked as though they would snap if you touched them.'

'It sounds very interesting,' Lucy said, pushing her bowl away, her soup still half-eaten. 'Tell me about the work you do.'

'I create many of the designs for our family business, but I also spend too much time in the furnaces. Which is a necessary evil.' His full lips lifted in a smile—the first time she had seen him smile. She held his gaze as he continued. 'I am the youngest son, and my father has always insisted that each of us learn every aspect of the business. My oldest brother, John, has no interest and he has a dairy farm ten miles away along the coast. Jacob, my other brother, has much more interest in the business side of the factory and has managed to get many export contracts. My father is very proud of him, after his disappointment of John taking on our grandparent's farm.'

'And you, young Tom,' she asked softly. 'Is he proud of you?'

He lowered his gaze. 'I think he would prefer me to be more hands-on, but I much prefer designing our pieces. Much of our work—and what

Jacob would prefer we focus on—is the production of kitchenware to supply the London stores.'

'It sounds very interesting.' Lucy had smothered a yawn. Ever since she had come to beside the stones, her head had been fuzzy and she'd been sleepy. It had been hard to stay awake as Tom had carried her through the fields to Glastonbury.

'I will escort you to your room.' He stood and came around to her side of the table and helped her stand. Lucy smoothed her hands down her cheesecloth pants. Her white trousers and Roman sandals had garnered some curious looks as they had come through the hotel into the small dining room.

'Thank you, I'm tired.' Her voice shook as she thought about what had happened. Maybe this was all a dream and she'd wake up in the cottage with Joshua snuggled into her back, his little chest rising and falling as he slept.

'And try to sleep, Lucy,' he had said at the door. 'Tomorrow we will go to the cottage and get things sorted for you.'

'Thank you, Tom. You are a very kind man.'

Now she crossed quickly to the door and opened it a crack. 'I just woke up. What time is it?'

***

Tom looked at the sleep-flushed face and the tousled hair of the beautiful woman who peered around the door at him.

'It's just gone eight o'clock. They will only serve breakfast for a short time.'

'I'm not hungry. I'd like to go to the cottage now.'

He nodded. 'I'll wait in the foyer.'

'I'll just have a quick wash.'

'Very well.' As Thomas walked down the stairs to the bottom floor of the hotel, he cursed himself for being so tongue-tied in Lucy's presence. Despite her circumstances—and he was still unsure what they were—she appeared to be an intelligent woman of class.

He was keen to find out more about her, and where she came from. Her accent was very different and he wondered if she'd come from one of the Eastern European countries. He hadn't recognised the term she had used earlier. Aussie? Perhaps Austria?

He waited in the foyer, his hands in his pockets and his head down wondering what to do. Could he afford the time to spend a few more days here with her, if they couldn't find what she was looking for? He couldn't leave her until she was home and safe.

'I'm ready,' a soft voice said behind him.

Tom spun around.

Lucy still wore the same clothes—of course she did, he reminded himself—but she had pulled her hair from her face and tied it back. Large brown eyes fringed with dark lashes looked at him solemnly.

'I am ready to go.'

'Would you share a pot of tea with me first?'

She nodded. 'Okay.'

Those strange words she used.

He led the way to the dining room and held her chair so she could sit down.

'Thank you,' she said quietly.

They sat without speaking until a young woman in a maid's uniform came from the kitchen and took a pot of tea, a small jug of milk, two cups and saucers and a rack of toast from the tray and placed them in the middle of the table.

Lucy waited until she was gone and picked the pot up. 'Shall I pour?' A small smile crossed her face briefly. 'I'm starting to talk like you.'

'Like me?' he said, raising his brows.

'More formally. I guess that's the way you speak here.'

'I am not from here. I am from Cornwall,' he reminded her. Perhaps she had forgotten what he had told her yesterday.

'Yes, I remember, but if I told you what I meant, you would think I'd lost the plot.' Her voice lowered. 'Maybe I have.'

'The plot? The garden was different too?'

Her chuckle was low. 'No. I guess that's a phrase that isn't around yet.'

'I don't understand.'

'Where I come from to lose the plot means . . . ' She tipped her head to the side and her pretty lips tipped up again in a smile. She was a beautiful woman, but when she smiled her whole face lit up. 'To lose the knack to understand what's happened or to cope with things, to go off the rails. But I guess that means nothing too. Just ignore me. If I told you what had really happened, I guess you'd run a mile.'

Sympathy flooded through him at the sadness on her face. 'Perhaps you could try me out and trust me with your story.'

'I'll pour our tea first,' she said.

'And I shall butter you some toast.' There were pats of butter and little bowls of conserve on the table. 'You need to keep your energy up.'

'Milk or black tea?' she asked holding the jug up.

'Milk please.'

'First or last? Red-headed kids or not?' This time, her smile was cheeky.

'I beg your pardon?' he asked with a frown.

'I'd forgotten, but Alice reminded me of the old wives' tale. My mum used to say it too. Milk goes in last, and you have red-headed kids.'

'These days it doesn't matter,' he replied holding up the white cup. 'Before we had porcelain cups, the milk was added first to stop the fine china from cracking.'

'I guess that makes sense.' A slight frown marred her smooth brow as he put the cup down and she poured the tea into it. 'You know if it wasn't for my worry about Joshua, my little boy—if I knew he was all right—I could enjoy being here. I could learn so much.'

'Pour your tea, and have some toast,' he pushed the plate over to her, 'and we will go and find out what has happened.'

'I know what has happened. I just need to find out how to fix it.' Tom was pleased when Lucy reached for a piece of toast and nibbled on it.

'So tell me what has happened.'

With a small sigh, Lucy sat back and put her cup down on the saucer with a soft clink. 'Will you promise to stay with me until we get to the cottage, even though you may think I am crazy.'

'Even if I think you have "lost your plot"?' he asked with a smile. Tom couldn't help it. Despite her situation—whatever that was—he had not been this interested in a young woman before. She was vibrant and alive, and even beneath her worry and sadness, a sense of humour shone through.

'Yes, even though you might think that.' She took a deep breath. 'I came to visit my Aunt Alice in Violet Cottage two weeks ago. I came from a long way away. From what I guess you would call the colonies. I don't know my history well enough to know what Australia is called in 1851.'

'Ah, that makes sense. Your strange dress and your different way of speaking.'

'In a way,' she said. 'Anyway, this is where it gets a bit crazy. The "woo woo" music kicks in.'

She looked up at him and Tom realised he must have been looking at her strangely because she chuckled again. 'The women in our family are a bit special.'

'Special?'

'Have I lost you?'

'Yes, a little. Woo woo?'

She stood suddenly and put her cup down. 'Come on, can we please go now? I will explain more after we've been to the cottage.'

Tom stood and came around and took her arm. 'Take a breath, Lucy. It will be all right. We will find out what has happened.'

Her eyes were wide as she looked up at him, and the strangest feeling suffused his chest.

'Do you trust me?' she asked.

'I believe I do. The question is do you trust me?'

'Strangely I do,' she said with a sad smile.

Chapter Ten

Glastonbury, 1851

Lucy put her trust in Tom as they walked down the road, taking a different route to the way they had come into Glastonbury. He had settled the account for the rooms and the breakfast, and she knew whatever happened today, she would be forever grateful to him. His kindness and his concern for her had been extraordinary. He had asked the maid in the dining room if she knew Violet Cottage and she had given them directions to get to the village of Pilton by the main road, and then take a different route to the cottage. Lucy remembered when she and Joshua had taken the cab from the station to Alice's cottage, they had driven through a village called Pilton.

Maybe she was being naïve, but Tom was very different to Royden.

'I know it well,' the young maid had said, her cheeks flushed as she smiled shyly at Tom. Lucy could understand why, he was a good-looking man, and his voice held a deep timbre that was very appealing. 'When you get to the crossroads, take the left road and then a mile along you will see the lane with two cottages. Violet Cottage and Rose Cottage. My grandmother lives in Violet Cottage.'

Lucy had interrupted. 'You know the McLarens in Violet Cottage?'

The maid shook her head and kept her eyes on Tom. 'No, I know of her. The cottage is often empty. I know that because my gran minds the cat when she is away.'

'Her?'

'Miss McLaren. Her name is Thelma, and she and my gran went to school together

I wonder if that was the woman at the cottage yesterday? Lucy thought.

They followed the directions the young girl had given and took the left road.

'There,' Tom said. 'Is that the cottage? Your cottage?'

Lucy drew a deep shuddering breath as she looked ahead. It was Alice's cottage, but it wasn't. Smoke curled lazily from the chimney, and as they approached Lucy could see how it was different. When she had gone to the door yesterday she had been in too much of a state about finding Joshua to pay attention to the cottage. Now, as she looked at it more closely, she could see the differences that had occurred over the years. Just small changes, but it was definitely the same cottage at a different time.

'It is. It is my aunt's cottage, but I know now she isn't there, like the woman who was there yesterday told me.'

'Someone is there, as there is smoke coming from the chimney.'

'That's from the woodstove in the kitchen at the back.'

'Would you like me to speak to them, or shall you?' Tom asked with a frown. He looked concerned and she wondered if he was preparing himself for her disappointment

'I will. But it will be very good to have your support. I do appreciate it, and I know I have led you a merry dance when you probably intended going back to your journey today.'

'Very well. I shall be there for you.' He smiled and a little quiver tugged at her belly as he held her gaze. Lucy found it hard to look away from the intensity of his eyes. 'I have been away from home for two months, one or two days more shall make no difference.'

'Thank you, Tom.' Lucy put her arm through the crook of his elbow. 'You are a good man. A rare find.' She knew she had to stop the attraction she was beginning to have to this man; it was only because he had been so kind to her and was looking after her. It had nothing to do with his sexy voice and how good-looking he was. She had made enough mess of her life already; that was why she was in Violet Cottage with Aunt Alice—to try to sort out her future.

Or why she *had* been in Violet Cottage.

That cottage now loomed in front of her as they approached, and cold fear settled in the pit of Lucy's stomach. This cottage held the key to her returning home, and to getting back to Joshua. There had to be someone who could help her if what Alice had told her was true. Someone with knowledge of the stones; if not, she couldn't bear to think about what would happen.

Her stomach churned with nerves, and she bit her lip until it hurt.

Tom opened the tall wooden gate and the rusted hinges creaked loudly as he pushed it far enough for her to step through. A curtain twitched at the window, and his hand slid down her arm and he took her hand in his. 'I can feel you shaking, Lucy. Be calm. All will be well.' He raised his other hand and knocked on the wooden front door. He stepped back a little but still kept hold of her hand.

The door opened slowly, and the same woman Lucy had spoken to yesterday stood there. 'Good morning, I'm sorry to bother you again, madam, but

I needed to come back and get some more information from you.'

The woman's face was lined and she didn't smile, but her eyes held kindness. 'I told you yesterday, there is no Alice McLaren here, and I know of no one called Alice.'

Lucy nodded. 'I know that now, but I was hoping to speak to you. I need to ask some questions. You are Thelma?'

'No. That is my husband's sister. I am a McLaren by marriage only.' The woman shook her head slowly. 'We are staying in Thelma's cottage for a short time until we move to Wales to live with our son.'

'Is she here?' Lucy asked eagerly. 'Thelma?'

'No, she's gone away.'

'Do you know when she'll be back?'

'Yes, in one month. Midsummer. She has gone to Scotland.'

Lucy closed her eyes. 'Are there any other family members close by? I must speak to a McLaren woman.' She pulled her hand from Tom's and clenched both hands in front of her imploring the woman to help her. 'I must. It is a matter of life and death. Please.'

The woman's glance held sympathy as she looked from Lucy to Tom, but she shook her head. 'I'm sorry, miss, but there is only Thelma and

James in the family. If you want to speak with her, you will have to come back in July.'

The door closed slowly, and Lucy began to tremble.

'My God, what am I going to do?' Her breath burned as she drew in deep gasps. 'I have to find out how to get home. I can't wait a month. I can't leave Joshua for that long.'

Tom reached for her as she began to shake all over before her knees gave way. His hands went to her shoulders and he held her steady. 'Breathe slowly and evenly, Lucy. The first thing you are going to do is tell me exactly what has happened and why you need to speak to that particular woman, and then we will make a plan.'

'I have nowhere to go, and I have no money. I have no clothes apart from what I am wearing.' Lucy's voice hitched in a sob. 'I have nothing, and she is the only one who can tell me how to get home.'

Tom looked at her thoughtfully, but his brow was wrinkled with confusion 'You have no family here? Apart from your Aunt Alice and your child who appear to have gone missing? And this Thelma is the only one who knows how to find them?'

'I know it sounds strange, but I cannot tell you what happened because you'll think I am mad.' Lucy put her hand to her mouth. Her stomach was still churning, and the toast she had eaten in the hotel a couple of hours ago seemed to be stuck in her throat. 'That is the gist of it. But my God, I can't wait a month. I have no money to get to Scotland, and if I did go there, I wouldn't know where to find her.'

She put a hand to her mouth. 'And if she's a true McLaren then perhaps she has travelled far away as I have?'

Tears welled in her eyes, and a sob caught in her throat. 'What if I never find out how to go home? Oh, Tom, what if I never see my little boy again?'

Chapter Eleven

Glastonbury, 1851

As they walked down the lane away from the cottage that had not provided an answer to Lucy's dilemma, Tom began to formulate a plan. Lucy clung tightly to his hand, and it felt . . . right. He could help her, and she could help him. It seemed to be the only solution; the woman she needed to see was not going to be here for a month. He knew she was upset; Lucy hadn't spoken since she had mentioned the little boy who was missing.

She said she had nowhere else to go. Tom was making an assumption about her situation, and if he was wrong, his plan would not be feasible. He had a solution, but he wasn't sure if he should broach it to her while she was upset, or if it would be better to wait.

But time was of the essence; he had already spent more time here than he had planned. He glanced across at Lucy; she held her head high and her eyes were clear. A rosy flush stained her cheeks, and she seemed to be deep in thought.

But there were no tears.

Finally, they reached the crossroads and he turned to her. 'What are you thinking, Lucy?'

Despite her earlier distress, her voice was steady. 'I have pulled myself together as I realised I have to find somewhere to stay for the next four weeks. I cannot stay out here like a homeless person, and I have nowhere else to go until my . . . until my relative returns from Scotland. I am trying to think of what I can do. How I can earn some money and find some lodgings.' She looked down at her apparel. 'And some clothes and shoes.'

He kept his voice quiet and gentle. 'I have a suggestion that I would like you to consider. It will give you somewhere to live for a month and one that will solve a dilemma that I am returning home to in my town.'

'And that is?'

He shook his head. 'I noticed a tearoom as we left town. You need to eat to keep your strength up.'

'You can't keep feeding me and paying for everything, Tom. That's not fair. Surely there is some work I could do in the town? In Glastonbury? I could do what that maid was doing at the inn. I had some waitressing experience before—' She cut her words off in mid-sentence, and then looked at him. 'Before Joshua was born.'

'We can sort that out later. For the time being, come with me. Humour me, and listen to what I have to say. If you think'—he smiled at her—'that I have "lost your plot" as you call it, you can tell me. But I see it as a solution for you for the month you have to wait, and for me on my return to St Austell. Will you listen to what I have to say?'

'I will.' Her gaze was intense as she nodded.

***

Even though Tom's words came as a shock to her, Lucy stayed quiet as she listened to him. What he had to say made sense, and although she had only known him for less than a day, she knew innately that he was a trustworthy young man, and that he wasn't trying to take advantage of her.

Young man? she wondered.

When he began to outline his plan, Lucy tipped her head to the side and stared at him over her cup of tea. 'My first question. How old are you, *young* Tom?'

'I am twenty-seven years old. How old are you, Lucy?'

'I am twenty.'

She picked up the cup of tea that had been brought to her by the older woman with a kindly face.

'I have another question for you, Lucy. Tell me if I am out of line, but I need to know. Ah,' he hesitated as she watched him carefully, and she waited for him to continue. When he did, his words did not surprise her. 'Where is your husband?'

She stared at him for a long time, wondering if he would understand her situation.

'I do not have a husband.' She held up her hand and showed her bare ring finger. 'I have a partner, but we are currently apart. Let me explain. When our little boy was born, we were engaged to be married, but a couple of things happened and I decided I didn't want to commit yet.' His eyes held hers. 'I know that might be difficult for you to understand. And I am sure, here and now, that being an unmarried mother is a stigma, but it is very different where I come from.'

'Will you change your mind and marry the father of your child?'

She shrugged. 'To be honest? I don't know. I don't think so. I need to have a husband I can trust, and if I can't trust, there is no point. I cannot trust Joshua's father. When I discovered he had been two-timing me—'

'Two-timing?' Tom interrupted with a frown. 'I am not familiar with that term.'

'He has shown me more than once he is not to be trusted. He has another woman in his life. He has done it before, and now he has done it again. That is why we are over here visiting my aunt. To give me time away from him, time to think. He has promised to never do it again, but my trust has been broken.'

'He is a very foolish man,' Tom said.

Lucy knew her smile was sad. 'He is. We have a beautiful little boy, and I have to trust that Joshua is safe with Aunt Alice.' Her breath caught as a thought came to her. 'Oh God, no. What if Aunt Alice contacts Royden, and he comes and takes Joshua?'

'Royden is his father?'

'Yes.'

'It would take him many weeks to travel here by ship, and your relative should be back within the month, from what the woman in the cottage said.'

Lucy tried to clear her head. The prospect of Alice calling Royden had thrown her into a spin, and she was less careful with her words than she had been before. 'Not now. You have to understand where I come from.' She looked back at him and held his gaze intently. Lowering her voice Lucy looked around, but the woman who had brought the tea had gone into the back room. 'If you get up and leave me after I tell you this, I will understand.'

'Tell me what?' His voice was as quiet as hers, but his eyes were kind.

'Tom?' Lucy couldn't help herself. She reached across the table and took his hands in hers. His skin was warm, but his fingers were rough and she could feel calluses on his palms. He had the hands of a craftsman.

'Please tell me, Lucy. I won't leave.'

'Okay. Here goes.' She drew in a deep breath. 'You know how I turned up near those stones?'

He nodded. 'Yes, I was walking along looking for the white clay bank, and you stumbled out from behind them.'

'I came *through* them,' she said quietly.

'Through them?' His face held a quizzical expression.

'Yes, where I came from is different, What you have to understand, it is not just *where*, it is *when*.'

This time Tom's mouth dropped open. 'When?'

'I told you how the women in our family are special?' Now that Lucy had decided to be truthful with him, she couldn't stop and the words raced from her lips. 'The women in our family apparently hold the key to travelling. We have a special ability to travel. We . . . um . . . leave where it is familiar and there is a place here where we can change the time we are in. Oh, how can I explain it.' Frustration laced her voice and she held his hands tightly. 'Look at me, Tom. You have surely noticed that my clothes are different. And my shoes.' She let go of one of his hands and held up her left wrist. 'And my watch? You said it had lost its hands. It never had hands, my watch has electronic numbers on it. There is no clock mechanism in it, it has a battery inside.'

'A battery?'

'Yes, a watch battery. I'm sure they weren't invented until the twentieth century.'

He took his hand away from her grip. 'The twentieth century? That is fifty years into the future.'

Lucy nodded and held her breath, praying that he wouldn't think she was mad.

He reached for his tea and closed his eyes as he drained the cup.

Putting it down, he nodded back at her. 'That is why you speak differently, and why your aunt and your little boy aren't at the cottage. They are at the cottage, but not now.'

Lucy couldn't help the tears that sweet relief brought. 'Exactly! You understand. Oh, Tom, you understand exactly what I am saying. Thank you.'

'And this woman who is coming back from Scotland will be able to help you?'

'Aunt Alice told me all about the travel last week, and I must admit I was sceptical. She's always been the eccentric in our family, and she told me of her travel to a much earlier time, back in medieval days, where she *said* she spent thirty years in a manor with her husband from that time. A manor called Brue Manor, and her husband's name was Branton. She said that this ability to travel is passed down through the men and women in the family—but only the women seem to travel. She didn't have a lot of detail, because she doesn't understand it as well, but she showed me her diaries, and, as crazy as it sounds I believe her.' Lucy shook her head from side to side. 'I have to believe her because look at me now. Here I am with you in Glastonbury in 1851.' She shook her head. 'Unless, of course, I am dreaming.'

'No, you are not dreaming, Lucy. You are sitting opposite me, and yes we are in a tearoom in Glastonbury in 1851. Tell me, where were you before I saw you at the stones?' he asked. 'Or perhaps I should say *when* were you?'

'Oh, dear Tom. You understand. How lucky was I that it was you in the field yesterday!' Lucy's hands were shaking as she reached out to hold his hands again. His fingers curled around hers, and she felt at ease for the first time in almost twenty-four hours. 'To answer your question. I came from 1989. Now the problem I have to solve is how to get back there. Or should that be then?'

Chapter Twelve

Glastonbury, 1851

Tom had heard of the mythical magical lines that connected Glastonbury to St Michael's Mount in Cornwall, not far from his home in St Austell.

'It's not a new concept to me,' he said. Lucy's fingers were ice cold in his. 'In this time—our time—the places where people can journey as you have, are called fairy paths.'

Lucy's eyes widened and her lips tilted in the most beautiful smile. 'You said, "like I have?" You believe me?'

A surge of affection for this lovely woman hit Tom square in the chest. What sort of man would choose another woman over her, especially when she had carried and given birth to his child? The thought made him sick to the stomach.

'I do. I see no reason for you to lie. And Lucy, I only have to look at you to know that you are not from our time. The way you hold yourself with such confidence. The distress when you talk of your young boy. The way you dress, the way you speak. I do believe what you say.'

Their eyes locked, and Lucy's smile got wider. Tom found it hard to look away; he was drowning in her eyes.

Her hand held his tightly as she nodded at him again. 'Thank you. Thank you so much for believing me, and accepting me for what I am, Tom. You have no idea what strength that gives me to know that someone is supporting me and helping me. Tell me about these fairy paths.'

'I don't know a lot about them, but I have heard of them. They join points of significance, and I have heard of journeys through time.' He smiled at her. 'But you are the first traveller I have encountered.'

'Excuse my language, or blasphemy, or whatever you call it these days, but holy shit, Tom, this is the first time I've travelled!'

He couldn't help laughing, and they must have made enough noise to attract attention because the teashop owner came across to the table.

'Would you like more tea?' she asked with a gentle smile.

Lucy nodded. 'Yes, please, and I have my appetite back. May we have some morning tea?'

'I have some Eccles cakes just coming out of the oven.' The woman pressed her hand on Lucy's wrist. 'It is good to see you smile, dear.'

A fresh pot of tea and a plate of delectable smelling pastries were placed in front of them. Tom was feeling much more comfortable with Lucy's reactions, and relief hit when she sat back and stared at him.

'Right, young Tom, we have all of that out of the way, now tell me this idea you have.' Her voice held much more confidence than it had before.

'Very well.' He reached for a pastry, more to delay his words than from any hunger.

He chewed slowly and he could sense Lucy's impatience as she folded her arms.

'So? Are you going to leave me hanging all day?'

'Hanging?'

'Waiting!' she said.

He looked around, and they were alone in the room again. 'Very well. The idea I have had, will give you somewhere safe to live for the next month while you wait for your relative to return. It will also help me out of a bind.' He hesitated and swallowed. 'It will give me good reason not to marry the woman who is determined I will be her husband.' He swallowed and then forged on. 'I propose that you marry me and that you then live in my house for four weeks, before I return you to Glastonbury.'

'Whoa! Stop right here. I'm not going to get in the way of your girlfriend. I am certainly not going to play the other woman. I've had enough of all that already, thank you very much!'

'Hush,' Tom said. 'Let me explain. It will not be a real marriage. It will just suit our purposes very well. You will have lodgings and money, somewhere to stay for the month. Somewhere you will be safe. I will be able to continue my life as I see fit, and have a reasonable excuse to stop Isabelle from thinking she is going to be my wife. Trust me, Lucy. You will see when—if—you meet Isabelle, what I mean. She is not the woman I want for my wife. My family are pressuring me—'

'Why would they do that?'

'Because her father is an astute businessman with many contacts throughout the country and abroad, and *my* father sees that as being beneficial to the factory.'

Lucy put her head to the side and then quietly placed her teacup in the saucer. Tom still hadn't seen her eat anything. 'We need to discuss what will happen if I accept this proposal of yours. I have some questions.'

'Please ask them and I will do my best to answer. Trust me I will answer honestly.'

'Okay. One, when will we get married and where? Two, what will you do in a month when I have gone? What reason will you give? And three . . . what sort of marriage will this be? Am I expected to be your wife in all aspects? You know, what do you call it now? Consummated? In the biblical sense?'

Tom's face heated and he knew it would be bright red. 'Um, n...no. The thought had not come to me, but no. You already have a partner and you are a mother. So, no! Of course not. It will be a marriage in name only.'

'I guess if the law is the same now, it means you can get the marriage annulled, and then you'll be free to marry whoever you want in the future.' Lucy nodded slowly. 'And the rest. If I agree, what is the when and where?'

Tom thought for a while. He had no idea what was needed to arrange a legal marriage in a town away from his home. 'Let me give my proposal more thought. Perhaps I was too hasty in suggesting we truly marry. Even though it is dishonest, perhaps it may be easier to pretend that we are married. I would hate to further complicate your life by sending you back to your time beholden to me.'

'Would that work? Would your family believe that you would go away for a short while and come back married?'

'My family do not understand me well. I have always been a misfit, much more interested in the creative side of the business. Over the past year or so, I have learned to be more assertive. So, no, they will not be surprised. Disappointed, but not surprised. And I have been away for over two months, so that is plenty of time to—'

'To meet a woman, fall in love and get married.'

'Yes.'

'But surely they appreciate you? And you can make your own decisions?' Lucy seemed to be having trouble accepting what he said.

'Previously no. Being away in London at the exhibition has made me value my independence more. To do what *I* want. What matters to me. What is important in my life. For a short time, I even considered moving to Germany and working with the craftsmen there to hone my skills.'

'But you changed your mind?'

'Yes, I did. After much thought. For the present time I am needed in the family business, and I will honour my family, but I have learned much about myself while I was away. They will find a great change in me even if I go home alone.' He smiled. 'Coming home with a wife will help to convince my father that I am a man of decision.'

'And show the woman who wants to marry you that you are no longer on—what did they call it then? I mean now? The marriage market?' Lucy held his gaze, and he found it impossible to look away. 'I think you are a very honest man, Tom.'

'I try to lead a good life,' he said simply, and then he couldn't help the smile that crossed his face. 'For me to suggest such a solution to you is very much out of character for me. But Lucy, your situation has touched me, and in all honesty, I could not go back to St Austell and leave you here to fend for yourself while you wait for this woman to return. If you do not want to accept what I have offered, I understand. I will stay here in Glastonbury and wait with you for the month.'

Lucy sat straight and he could almost see the thoughts running through her mind as she continued to stare at him.

Disappointment jarred through Tom when she took her hand away and looked down. She picked up her cup and sipped slowly.

He waited, wondering what he could do to persuade her.

'No,' she finally said.

'Then I will stay here with you.'

'No. I would not expect you to do that.' Her smile was sweet. 'I meant I will come to St Austell, and I will pretend to be your wife until it is time for me to leave. But there is one condition.'

Tom held back the words that fought to come from his lips. '*Anything*,' he had been about to say before common sense prevailed. 'And what would that be, Lucy?'

Chapter Thirteen

Violet Cottage, March - 2019

Lucy sat outside Violet Cottage with Beth. Daffodils and snowdrops and tiny violets had appeared in the garden over the past few days as spring began to warm the cold ground. Megan and David had gone back to Scotland, and Silas had gone to London, telling Beth that he needed to pick up a new guitar, but Lucy suspected it was to give her time alone with her daughter. Silas was a good man, and it was clear that he loved Beth very much. Knowing that both her children had partners who loved them made the prospect of her journey ahead easier.

The conversations she had had with her daughter over the past two days had been difficult. Not so much that Beth had been upset learning that Royden was not her true father, but more because Lucy was going back to look for her Thomas, and if she found him, she would consider staying.

'Mum, you haven't thought this through,' Beth said. 'It's been how many years? Almost thirty? The chances are, he is married and has a family.' She put a hand to her mouth and her words broke Lucy's heart. 'And if he does, I could have more brothers and sisters.'

Lucy swallowed and held back the tears. 'I know that, Beth. But I have to know. I see how much you love Silas, and I know how much Alice loved her Branton. I had that same love in my life for such a short period, and I've waited thirty years before I allowed myself to try to find Thomas again. Beth, I have to. I want you to understand.'

'Why did you wait so long, Mum?'

'It was simple. I had you and Joshua to consider.'

'But we've both been gone from home for almost ten years. If you wanted to go back, why wait until now?'

'Because I carried so much guilt. I had a misplaced loyalty to Royden. He wasn't all bad, Beth. He provided for us, and he tried to be a good father. We had some good years together.'

Beth pulled a face. 'Yeah, but he failed miserably as a true life partner. How many affairs has he had over the years, Mum? I could never understand why you turned a blind eye.'

'Well,' Lucy said briskly. 'It might have taken me a while to wake up, but I have now and I am going to do what I want to do. Someone said to me once that they were going to do what *they* wanted. What mattered to *them*. What was important in their life.' Lucy stared over the back garden to the stones glowing in the late afternoon sunshine. Her voice was soft. 'He did, and it showed me how happiness is made. I want that again, Beth. Or I want to see if it's still there. When I was young, I had confidence, and I looked forward to the future. Tom said he would wait for me to come back, and I have to take that on trust. I promised him that I would when I could, if I could, and I've made him wait a very, very long time.'

'Mum, do you know how scary this all is? If Silas hadn't followed me, I'd still be wandering around in the medieval past trying to find my way home.'

'I know, Beth, but I'm prepared to take that risk. Alice taught me so much when I came back. How to go to where I want to travel, arrive in the right place and at the right time. All the things I didn't know when I accidentally went through and met your father.'

'How did she know all that, Mum? I've read her diaries and journals, but there's so much she didn't write down.'

'There was. And I promise I'll tell you before I go, Beth. I'll pass the knowledge on to you, but I want you to promise me that you'll use that knowledge very wisely if you use it at all.'

'When will you go?' Beth's lip quivered.

'I will stay with you for a week. I have some preparations to make before I go.' Lucy stood and walked around to Beth's chair. She stood with her hands on her shoulders and then bent and placed her cheek against her daughter's. 'We'll have a happy week, and I will tell you about your father. You are very much like him, sweetheart.'

'Did he ever see me?'

Lucy shook her head. 'No. No, he didn't.'

'Have you Googled him?' Beth's question took Lucy by surprise.

'What good would that do?'

Beth shook her head. 'Mum, are you still a technophobe? Do you ever use the internet? Do you know how much information's out there?'

Lucy pulled a face at her daughter. 'I pay my bills online and I use email. And I have my mobile phone. That's all I need.'

'Mum, do you know you can join ancestry sites and find the birth, death, and marriage certificates going back hundreds of years? And if . . . if my father did anything famous, there could even be a record of it on the internet.'

'No,' Lucy said as she walked back around to her chair 'There couldn't be. We're talking over close to two hundred years ago.'

'Mum.' Beth's voice held extreme patience. 'At worst, we can find out the date of his death. And then it may save you that trip through the stones.'

Lucy froze as Beth pulled out her phone. 'What are you doing?'

'I'm putting him into Google. I have a right to search for my father,' she said defensively. Her fingers flew over the keys. 'Tell me something more about him. Where did he live? What did he do?'

Lucy stared out over the back garden and the high stone wall that Alice said her parents had built back in the 1930s to keep *her* away from the stones. The afternoon light was fading quickly and it wouldn't be long before the time gate opened at sunset, and the stones emitted the bright blue flash that Alice had told her happened at the moment of sunrise, sunset, and noon each day. She thought of Tom, and the first time she had seen him as she stumbled from behind the stones.

'He was a potter,' she said softly. 'His full name was Thomas Egbert Adams. He hated his middle name but, it was a family tradition. They called him young Tom.'

'Having his full name should make him easier to find. How old was he and what year was it?'

'It was 1851 and he was twenty-seven. So that would make his birth date around 1824.'

'And yesterday, you told me you went to Cornwall with him. Where to?' Beth asked.

'A town on the coast called St Austell.'

Lucy leaned back and lifted her face to the weak sunshine as Beth peered at her phone.

'I'll find something, Mum. Give me half an hour.'

Chapter Fourteen

St Austell, Cornwall - 1851

Lucy sat primly in the seat by the window of the train, taking little notice of the other two women in the carriage. They had boarded at Exeter, and she and Tom had stopped discussing what they would do. They had created a past for Lucy, how they had met, how her family lived in Morocco, and how they had married in the General Register office in Somerset House. To Lucy's surprise, Tom had suggested they change her age to twenty-five as he said it was unusual for a girl of twenty to marry.

'It's unusual enough that you are away from your family.'

'In Morocco,' she said with a smile.

His grin had sent a quiver to her nether regions, and then she'd smiled again. She was getting the hang of the language of the nineteenth century.

Lucy crossed her ankles and then reached down and pulled her dark brown skirt down to cover her stockings. Stockings that made her skin prickle and itch, but she could put up with that. Not that she had settled into her character, but she was fascinated with everything she saw, and the next four weeks was sorted. The carriage had held three couples when she and Tom had boarded the train at Glastonbury, and then from Taunton to Exeter they had been alone.

Thanks to Tom agreeing to her one condition—that he take her shopping and buy clothes that assisted her to blend in—Lucy knew she no longer stood out. She smiled as she recalled the relief on his face when she had told Tom her one simple condition. Now, she had to learn to act like a woman of the nineteenth century so she would fit into Tom's life until he brought her back to Glastonbury in four weeks. She had a small wardrobe that would be sufficient to get her through the next month without standing out like a sore thumb.

Yesterday before they had left the tearoom, Tom had asked the kind woman there for assistance in purchasing some new clothes for his "sister". Mrs Mowbray, as she had introduced herself, had directed them to her sister's shop not far from the hotel they had stayed in.

Tom had escorted her to the shop, explained that his "sister" needed some skirts and blouses and shoes, and waited outside while she was attended to and then had paid for the lot.

The look in Tom's eyes when she had walked out onto the street, in a brown skirt and white buttoned-up blouse, with her hair pulled neatly back, had sent a tingling through her. It was happening way too often for her comfort.

She owed Tom so much; that's all this feeling was. Gratitude. He was quiet and kind, and very concerned for her well-being. He had given his word that he would bring her back to Glastonbury so she could find out how to go home, back to Alice's cottage in the right time, and back to Joshua. She pushed back the shiver of worry that ran down her back. If Joshua had followed her, he would have been next to her when she came to in the field. She had to trust that he was safely with Aunt Alice. And she was safely with Tom, being taken care of very well. It had been her lucky day that he had been in the field when she had arrived. God knows what would have happened to her if he hadn't been there.

Lucy trusted him, and in return she would do as much as she could to help him. As they had waited at the station for the train to Cornwall, she had peppered him with so many questions about St Austell, his family, Isabelle—who she had already decided she wouldn't like—Tom had put his hands up and laughed.

'You make my head spin, Lucy.' He reached down and picked up the small carpetbag that he had insisted on buying to put her clothes in. 'Come, I heard the train whistle. It's not far off now. So, you must remember you are Mrs Adams now.'

Lucy touched her left hand and rubbed the plain gold band beneath the glove. Tom had purchased the ring at a jeweller's shop in the High Street after they had finished at the dress shop.

A strange feeling had overcome Lucy as they had sat in a small park and he had slipped it on her ring finger. She had looked up at him shyly, trying to hide the way her heart was racing, and reminding herself this was all play-acting.

With a huge whoosh of steam, the train roared into the station and she had grabbed for Thomas's arm.

Chapter Fifteen

St Austell, Cornwall - 1851

'Lucy?'

She jumped and woke as Tom's hand gently touched hers.

'We are almost to Plymouth.' His breath warmed her cheek.

She opened her eyes and his face was close to hers. A tingle ran down her back as she looked into the dark eyes that were becoming very familiar to her.

'Plymouth?'

'Yes, we will be met at Plymouth, most probably by my brother, John. I sent a message yesterday on the mail train to my father, when we went back to the hotel while you were resting before dinner.'

'Are they expecting me? Did you tell them anything?'

'No. We will have time to go back to my cottage, and we shall see them tomorrow. John is almost a recluse, and he will be pleased to meet you, but he won't see the rest of the family before we do.'

'I'm getting a bit nervous.' Lucy shook her head. 'And if you knew the real me, you would know that is way out of character. Nothing usually fazes me. Not before I arrived here and turned into a "married woman" about to meet my new family, not to mention, a woman who will hate me.' She tipped her head to the side. 'I like the idea of being a recluse, like your brother. That would make the four weeks here very easy. Can I do that?'

Tom reached out and took her hand and his fingers closed over her wedding ring. 'There is no need to be nervous. I have told you what my family think of me, and what Isabelle's desire was, but rest assured. You are in a totally polite family, and you will be treated with respect and kindness.'

'And curiosity,' she ventured.

Tom squeezed her hand. 'Yes, I am sure there will be curiosity.'

##

'I'm very pleased to make your acquaintance, Lucy.' Tom's brother was nothing like him in looks; fair-skinned and ruddy cheeks were surrounded by a thatch of thick fair hair. He pumped Thomas's hand. 'A big surprise, Thomas, but a good one. A good one, indeed. It will make Mother very happy.'

'Thank you.' Lucy put her head down and tried to focus on not sounding so Australian.

Tom held her arm as she stepped up into the cart behind two of the biggest horses she'd ever seen.

'It will be a bit more uncomfortable than the train, but the extension of the railway to St Austell has met with many holdups.' Tom gestured to a low seat in the back of the cart. It seemed to be covered with some sort of hessian sacking. 'You'll be more comfortable in there. I'll sit up the front with John.'

'How far is it to your home?'

'Just over thirty miles, so it will take the rest of the day to journey there.'

'Oh.' Lucy settled herself in the back of the cart and tried not to turn her nose up at the overpowering smell of horse manure on the ground where the horses had been standing. It was going to be a very long day. For the first time, doubt crept into her mind.

What have I agreed to?

Here she was in a cart in the south of England, hours away from the stones and the cottage, with two men she barely knew.

She took a deep breath, trying to convince herself that she wasn't making a stupid mistake. She could hear Royden's voice in her head. 'You never think things through Lucy, and you make some stupid decisions. It's one of the things about you that really annoys me.'

'Only one of them?' she had replied coldly.

She'd never forgiven Royden for that comment; he'd made it when she had told him she was pregnant, and she was too far along to have a termination. She should never have slept with him, but to his credit—about the only positive thing he'd done—he'd agreed to support her and they had moved in together.

'I'm sorry, babe. I'll be better when he grows bigger and I can talk to him and he can play sport,' was his constant response when she asked him to help more with Joshua. Finding out he had been seeing someone else had been the last straw after three years of virtually raising Joshua alone. She hadn't even told him she was going to England to stay with Aunt Alice until the taxi to take her to the airport was at the door.

And what had he said? 'And how the hell are you paying for that?'

Lucy had closed the car door in his face and refused to cry.

'Lucy?' Tom's quiet voice interrupted her musing. 'Are you comfortable? There is an inn about five miles ahead and we will stop for some refreshment.'

'I am good, thank you.' Lucy looked up into Tom's kind eyes and knew she had no reason to worry. She could do this for four weeks. Or almost four weeks as she had been here three days now, and it would take a couple of days to travel back to Glastonbury.

After three stops and a very long day, the light began to fade as dusk approached. An hour ago Tom had leaned over and pointed out John's farm as they went past it, and she had admired the fat healthy cattle that stood along the fence line.

'Not long now,' he said. 'My cottage is on this side of St Austell. We shall be there just on dark.'

Half an hour later, at sunset, the hooves of the two horses clopped on the cobblestones as they entered a small village. It was still light enough to see and Lucy looked around in awe. It was like one of those calendars of the Cotswolds that she'd loved. They passed a row of cottages with colourful gardens edged by emerald green grass. Ahead was a village green and the happy sounds of children playing broke the still evening air.

On the other side of the green, a larger cottage was set back from the paved road. A stone fence covered in lichen ran along the front. Lucy held onto the boards on the side of the cart as John called out 'Whoa,' and pulled the reins. The horses stopped and immediately began grazing on the lush grass at the edge of the road.

'We're home, Lucy,' Tom said.

John reached over and collected both of their bags, plus a small crate that she had noticed at her feet. Tom jumped down from the cart and held out both hands to her.

'I'll be getting along straight away and leave you two alone,' John said. He gestured to the crate he'd put on the ground next to the gate with their bags. 'There's milk and eggs, a cob of bread, and a slab of cooked mutton for you.'

'When did you start thinking about cooking, brother?'

Tom grinned as John's ruddy cheeks turned a deeper red. 'Ah, Mary heard you were coming home and she dropped that in for you last night.'

'That was very kind of her. Tell Mary we said thank you when you get home.'

John mumbled something indecipherable and then climbed up onto the bench. 'Aye, I will. I'm sure to see you as soon as Mother hears your news, young Thomas.' Lucy smiled when John winked at Tom. 'Now don't be forgetting to carry your wife over the threshold, brother.'

'Your turn next, brother,' Tom called after him as John clicked his tongue and the horses were off.

Soon the clopping of their hooves disappeared down the lane.

'What did you mean by that?' Lucy asked.

'Mary.' Tom smiled. 'My brother has been courting her for years. Looks like he's finally got a chance.'

Lucy shook her head. *Courting?* How different was life here? Not "let's meet up at a bar". Have a few drinks, listen to a band and then head off to bed. In the three days she'd spent here, she had noticed the slower pace of life and how pleasant it was. And how caring and interested people seemed to be in her well-being.

The gate creaked as Tom pushed it open and stood back to let Lucy walk in the front garden. She drew in her breath with a quick gasp as she looked at the beauty that surrounded her. Hollyhocks, lavender, magnolias, delphiniums, and marigolds—the garden was a riot of colour and sweet fragrance.

'Oh wow, how pretty is that!' she said.

'I like to be surrounded by beauty.' Tom lowered his voice. 'Please excuse my forward behaviour, Lucy, but Mrs Mapplethorpe is standing at her door with a broom and watching us.' He put the two bags and the crate he carried inside the door, and before Lucy could draw breath Tom had swept her off the ground and into his arms. 'It will soon get around the village that we are home, and if

I don't carry my bride over the threshold, it will be seen as strange.'

Chapter Sixteen

St Austell, Cornwall - 1851

Lucy's skin was still tingling where Tom's fingers had pressed against her when he had carried her into the cottage. He had ducked his head as they had come through the narrow doorway and closed the door with his foot before he put her down on the wooden floor.

He smiled down at her. 'Welcome to your home for the next four weeks, Lucy. I hope you will be comfortable here, and your visit is not too arduous. I'm sorry that I seemed to ignore you in John's cart, but it would have been uncomfortable for you upfront with us.'

'It was an experience,' Lucy said. 'It was interesting to look at the countryside as we travelled. It's so clean, no roads, no cars, no jet streams—' She broke off as she realised who she was talking to. 'Sorry, I forgot where I was for a moment.'

'No,' Tom said. 'Your time interests me. I would like to sit down with you and hear what the future is like.'

'I can't believe you've been so accepting of me. And you know what? So far I haven't missed anything. Apart from my little boy, of course.' Lucy took a deep breath. Joshua was in her thoughts constantly, and she wondered how he was coping without her. He was a confident child and he had taken to Alice as soon as they had arrived at Violet Cottage. 'The people here are kind, and the pace of life is so much slower. But it's the quiet I love.' She stifled a yawn.

'Oh, I'm sorry, Lucy. I gave no thought to you being tired from the journey. It was such an uncomfortable trip for you. I was expecting that John would have been in the family carriage, but apparently, Mother is down at Penzance visiting her sister.'

'She's away? Maybe I could just stay here, and we could hold off telling your family about being "married" until she gets home?'

'Perhaps, for a few days. It will give you time to get settled. Come, let me show you to your room, and around the cottage.'

Lucy smiled as Tom gestured for her to follow him through a narrow doorway. Again he ducked his head, and she noticed how low the ceilings were. Huge oak beams held up a whitewashed timber ceiling, and the walls were washed in the same white. The sofas and the table and chairs in the room he had taken her into were old fashioned like she had seen in historical homes she had visited.

'This was my father's parents' cottage and their grandparents' before them. I don't know how far it goes back, but it is the oldest cottage in the village.'

'And it's yours now?' Lucy asked as Tom bent down to light a lamp on the table.

'We lived here at Treffry when we were growing up. Until my father had success with the factory, and he built a new home for them overlooking the harbour. John took my other grandparents' farm when they passed on, and Jacob lives in a cottage on the factory grounds at West Polmear, so it was a given that I would stay in the family cottage.' He gestured to the next doorway. 'This is the scullery, and the way out to the back garden and the water closet, but follow me and I'll take you up to your room. Wait by the steps and I'll get your bag.'

A ripple of excitement ran through Lucy. As long as she had faith that she would be able to get back to Joshua and Alice, she would make the most of her weeks here. She pulled a face; it wasn't a surprise that Royden strayed from her thoughts and intentions.

'Is something wrong?' Light flickered around her as Tom appeared with her bag in one hand and another lamp in the other. He put the lamp on a table at the bottom of the steps and it threw the light upwards.

'No. I was just thinking. I'm fine. I am going to make the most of my time here, but I want you to tell me how I can help you. Apart from pretending to be your wife, I mean. I can cook, I can clean, and I can garden.'

In the dim light, Lucy could see the horror that crossed Tom's face.

'No, that would be totally inappropriate. I have a woman who comes in each day. She cleans and leaves my meal for when I come home from the factory.'

'And the garden?'

'My father's gardener gives me one day a week.'

'Oh. So what will I be expected to do?'

Tom rubbed a hand across the stubble on his face. With his dark hair and his olive skin, the afternoon shadow gave him a rakish look. 'You will be expected to visit and have guests once it is known you are my wife.'

This time, it was Lucy's turn to look horrified. 'Really? I thought I'd just have to deal with one meeting with your family. Is that entirely necessary?'

'That's the way things are done.'

'Done?' she asked. 'Do I have to?'

Tom shrugged. 'I guess not. It's just what is usually done. I hadn't thought much about that when I asked you to help me.'

'I suppose I can cope with chatting to a few people, it's not going to kill me. I just hope I don't make a fool of you. And what about Isabelle? Will I have to meet her?'

'Yes, eventually, but I will ensure that I am there for that meeting. If you are quiet and answer questions carefully, all will be well.'

Lucy tried to think back to all the period movies she'd seen. 'I don't know the right way to do things here. You'll have to teach me.'

Tom frowned. 'You are giving it too much thought. It will be known that you are from foreign climes and that you are used to different social settings. You will be a seven-day wonder, and then life will get back to normal.' He turned to go up the stairs. 'Be careful, the middle stair dips.'

When they reached the small landing at the top of the stairs, he reached over and opened a door, before lighting a lamp on the landing. 'This was the guest room when we all lived here, so it's quite clean and clear. Apart from the main bedroom, the rest of the floor is a storage area. Everything from when we three boys were growing up is stored in the rooms. I'll sleep in the room behind the parlour downstairs. I'll let you get settled, and then please come down when you are ready. I'll cut the bread and make a pot of tea unless you'd prefer a sherry?'

'Tea will be fine, thank you. I'll just lie down for a while and I'll be down soon.'

'Take this lamp into your room.'

Lucy waited until he'd gone downstairs and walked into the room where she would sleep for the next few weeks. It was very similar to her room at Aunt Alice's and looked out towards a mist-covered hill. The evening was coming in quickly and the eerie mist swirling into the valley sent a shiver down her back.

Sitting on the bed, she covered her face with her hands as doubt kicked in.

Had she made a huge mistake?

***

Tom lit the stove and unpacked the crate of food that Mary had sent with John. He looked at the fare he had placed on the cutting board and wondered what to prepare. He was hungry; they hadn't stopped for a meal because John had been keen to get home to his farm before dark. He'd organised for his farmhand to do the milking, as he had been gone for over half a day with the round trip to Plymouth and back.

Tom sliced some bread and cheese and added some slices of mutton to the platter as the kettle boiled on the stove. Walking to the back door, he looked out over the garden as he waited for Lucy to come down. He knew she was tired, and he'd sensed she was unsettled since they had arrived. Her concern about mixing with his family and others was unnecessary; she had interacted in a suitable way with him and those they had met at Glastonbury. He would reassure her as they ate.

Half an hour later, there was still no sign of her. Tom walked up the steps and tapped on the closed door.

'Lucy? I have a meal ready.'

There was no answer and Tom frowned. What if she'd decided it was too much and had fled?

Tapping on the door again, he waited and then turned the knob. He peered around the door, and let out the breath he'd held. Lucy was on top of the bed, her hand curled under a cheek as she slept. He walked across and spoke her name quietly but she didn't stir. Opening the chest at the foot of the bed, he took out a blanket and placed it over her, before carefully slipping her shoes off, then pulling the soft blanket over her stockinged feet.

Before he reached over to turn the lamp down—he didn't want her to wake through the night and wonder where she was—Tom stood at the side of the bed and looked down at his guest. Dark eyelashes fanned onto her cheeks which held a slight flush. Her lips were softly parted as she breathed deeply. A surge of protectiveness rose in him. Lucy was a beautiful woman, and he knew that the attraction that he felt to her was foolish. In four weeks, if all went to plan for her, she would leave and he would never see her again. He closed the door quietly as he went downstairs to partake of his solitary meal.

Chapter Seventeen

St Austell, Cornwall - 1851

Lucy snuggled into the soft pillow and pulled the blanket over her face, determined to go back to the sweet dream she'd been in the middle of when something had woken her up. She had put her hand up to Tom's face and he'd lowered his head and had been about to kiss her when a loud banging interrupted. Drifting back to sleep trying to catch the fragment of the dream, she groaned and opened her eyes when the banging started again.

Coming fully awake, she sat up.

What on earth am I doing dreaming about Tom?

She looked around at the unfamiliar room, and her gaze settled on the window. Grey scudding clouds raced across the glimpse of sky and raindrops splattered the glass.

And where am I?

With a shiver, she looked down and remembered that they had travelled to Tom's cottage yesterday. She had lain down for a rest and had gone out like a light. A lamp was still burning next to the bed, but it was obviously morning. She had gone to sleep and slept all night.

Lucy frowned again and swung her legs over the side of the bed as a loud bang came from below, followed by a voice. 'Thomas Adams. I know you are home, so open this door immediately.'

Lucy was still wearing the skirt and blouse she'd travelled in yesterday, and those awful rough scratchy stockings, but her shoes were by the side of the bed. She didn't recall taking them off. She'd kill for a hot shower, but she guessed she wasn't going to get one here. What did they do for hot water in 1851? Did it have to be heated over a fire?

God, who knew!

'Thomas!' The banging started again and this time the voice was shrill, and if it was possible, even louder. Lucy waited for Tom to open the door to his persistent visitor but all was quiet. As she stood, she noticed a piece of paper lying on the patterned carpet just inside the door. She walked over, picked it up and unfolded it.

Dear Lucy

I let you sleep, but I am sure you will be hungry when you wake up. I have gone to the factory for the morning. I have lit the stove, and the kettle is warm. There is food on the table. Please make yourself comfortable. I will be home for the midday meal. The fire is lit in the parlour, so you should be warm.

Yours sincerely
Thomas.

'Thomas!'

Lucy couldn't put up with the screeching any longer. Someone was after Thomas in a hurry. Slipping her new shoes on, she opened the door and made her way downstairs and through the parlour. There was another loud rat-a-tat at the door and she smoothed her hair back before she reached for the handle. The door opened and a plump girl with dark curly hair stared at her.

'Who are you?' she demanded rudely as she went to push past Lucy and go inside.

Lucy stood her ground and held the door with one hand, and the other side of the doorframe with the other. 'How may I help you?' She forced politeness into her tone, even though her temper had fired at the young woman's rudeness.

'I want to see Thomas.'

'And you are?'

The woman looked her up and down. 'What are you doing answering Thomas's door? I asked who you were!'

Lucy drew herself to her full height. Here goes, she thought.

'I am Lucy Adams. And you are?'

'Are you a cousin or something? I wasn't aware Tom had any *foreign* cousins.' The way she said "foreign" made it sound like an undesirable state. 'You have the look of his mother. Are you from that side of the family? Were you at the exhibition in London? Why did he bring you here? Why aren't you at the main house at the harbour?'

Lucy recalled a scene where Emma Thompson had played a haughty woman in a period movie she had once seen. The title escaped her memory, but she could picture the scene, and pulling herself straight and lifting her chin, she put on the poshest voice she could summon.

'You have many questions, miss, but your rudeness makes me loath to answer them. Perhaps if you showed some manners, I might tell you who I am.' A smile tugged at Lucy's lips but she refused to give in to it.

Put that in your pipe and smoke it, you rude little bitch.

A suspicion flared as she took a closer look at the young woman with her mouth now in a perfect O. 'Perhaps, miss, we could start again and make a proper introduction.'

The woman's eyes narrowed. 'I am Isabelle Lyndhurst and I am about to become betrothed to Thomas. Now, where is he? Kindly tell him I am here.'

Lucy let her eyebrows rise as she stared haughtily at the young woman, her suspicions confirmed. Thomas had had a lucky escape; she could see now why he didn't want to marry Isabelle Lyndhurst.

'I'm afraid my *husband* is not here.' She took great satisfaction at the dismayed reaction to her reply. 'But you are most welcome to come in and wait with me for his return. I am most interested to hear why you have the idea that Thomas was going to marry *you*.' Lucy knew she was being rude but she let her gaze run up and down the young woman in the same way she had been examined and dismissed.

'You're what? Don't be . . . you can't be . . . how can you say you have married my Thomas?' The rosy cheeks had blanched to white.

'Because he is obviously and never has been *your* Thomas,' Lucy said. She might be a bitch, but she was enjoying this unexpected confrontation. Getting it over and done with early was good. 'May I ask how you knew we had returned?'

The scowl deepened. 'Mrs Mapplethorpe's housekeeper told her daughter who is a maid at our manor.'

The housekeeper obviously wasn't there when Thomas had carried her over the threshold last night.

'I see. Would you like to come in?'

'No, I would not. I'm going to find Thomas!'

Lucy shrugged and closed the door without another word.

Reaction set in and she leaned her back on the door, wondering when Isabelle would find *her* Thomas.

Chapter Eighteen

St Austell, Cornwall - 1851

Tom hurried across the field and opened the back gate of the cottage, keen to check on Lucy. She must have come downstairs and stoked the fire because smoke was curling from the chimney. Anticipation ran through him as he opened the scullery door and entered the cottage.

Lucy was standing at the window and when she turned with a wide smile for him, Tom's stomach somersaulted. The talking to he had given himself about keeping his distance from her, on the walk back from the harbour had done him no good at all.

'Good morning,' he said, crossing the small room to take her hands in his. 'I see you have slept well. You look very bright this morning. Did you have some breakfast?'

'I did, thank you.' Her cheeks flared with more colour. 'I also had a visitor.'

'A visitor?'

'Yes. I made the acquaintance of your potential fiancée, Isabelle Lyndhurst, who told me *she* was about to become your betrothed.' Lucy looked down and he could have sworn she looked guilty.

'Oh, dear. I am sorry. I hope she didn't give you a difficult time. I am sure she would have wanted to know who you were.'

Tom's stomach somersaulted again as Lucy's pretty eyes danced.

'Oh, she did. And I told her.'

'You told her what?'

'That she couldn't be betrothed to you, because I was your wife.'

He gawked at her for a few seconds and then regained his composure. A chuckle bubbled up from his chest. 'Oh dear Lord, I would have loved to have seen Isabelle's face.'

'I am sure you will sooner or later because she strode off in a foul mood. She was very rude so I shut the door in her face. Last I heard was clomping footsteps down the path to the gate. She is *not* a nice person, and I can understand why you won't marry her.'

Tom's chuckle turned into a full-bellied laugh. 'Oh Lucy, I knew I was right to bring you home.' He squeezed her hands. 'She didn't upset you too much, did she?'

'No, not at all. Don't worry, I've dealt with a lot worse than a spoiled woman who can't get her way.' He wondered what she was thinking about as her mouth tightened and she stared out the window. 'Actually, after she left I almost felt sorry for her.'

'Almost?'

'Yes, then I remembered how rude she was to me.'

'I shall insist that she apologises to you.'

Lucy pulled her hands from his and shook her head. 'No, don't. I've seen her. She knows and I don't particularly want to see her again.'

Tom frowned 'She's not an enemy you would want to have, Lucy.'

'I don't really care, Tom. I'm only here for a month and she can't do anything to hurt me. Besides, it was good practice for me, and I coped very well. You would have been proud of the way I spoke. I felt as though I was in a movie.'

'A movie? I don't know what that means.'

'Sorry, I keep forgetting where I am. *When* I am. I feel as though you're part of my other life, and I forget that you don't understand where I came from. Many things are very different, but social stuff and relationships more than anything. That's why I was so nervous. Now that I've met Isabelle, I know I can handle myself, and make it seem as though I fit in. I can pull the "I'm from abroad card" if I have to. If I stuff up, I mean.'

'I only understood about half of what you said, but I think I understand the gist of what you're saying. Perhaps we can sit down and talk, and you can tell me about *your* time?'

'Shall I make a cup of tea?' Lucy burst out laughing. 'Oh, God, *shall* I? Normally I'd say "how about a cuppa!"'

'I have a lot to learn,' he said, loving the way her eyes crinkled when she laughed. The distant look had left her expression. 'And *I* feel as though I've known you for a long time too. I certainly won't forget you when you go to your home.' Tom found it hard to keep the smile on his face. 'And let's have a *cuppa*!'

***

Tom's eyes were like saucers as they sat at the table and Lucy told him about what life was like in 1989, an unknown future to him. The only thing she couldn't answer was his specific questions about his industry in the future. She told him about travel, and how quickly technology would progress in the next century. Looking around the cottage reminded her of each change that would be made to households, and she detailed the things that were basic to her but would make a huge difference to the way society lived here and now.

'I would love to visit you in your future,' he said.

'People are very different. Very focused on work, and stuff that gives them prestige. Fancy houses, cars. Investments, things like that. Things that make you look successful and rich. A culture of consumption is the term I've heard used.' Lucy smiled and shrugged. 'Who knows? It's happened in the movies. A couple of years ago, there was a movie called *Back to the Future*.'

'Movies? What's that?' Tom frowned.

Lucy wrinkled her nose and tried to think of the best description. 'Do you have cameras here yet? Photography?'

'I did see one at the exhibition in London, but I didn't linger. There was quite a crowd there. Tell me about them.'

'A camera captures images. Still or moving. Thus, they are called "movies". And you can look at it later. So we would take a picture of you and me, and we could capture a moment forever.'

Tom's expression softened. 'That would be nice for me to remember you after you go, but I'll have to keep you in my mind instead.'

Their eyes met and held and a swirl of attraction tingled through Lucy's nerve endings.

She dropped her gaze, pushing that constant attraction away. 'When we talk to Thelma when she comes back from Scotland, we might learn if that is possible. Oh, I wished I'd listened to Aunt Alice more carefully. If only she'd warned me, and told me how to get back, none of this would have happened.'

'I am pleased that it did, because otherwise, I wouldn't have met you.' Tom's voice held apology. 'I'm sorry, that was a selfish thing to say.'

'I'm pleased I met you, too,' Lucy said. She couldn't resist looking at him again. Even though she'd only known Tom for a few days, there was a deep attraction there. She knew she had to be careful, and not show him what she was feeling, but she could imprint his face into her memory too.

Totally crazy. It wasn't simply because he was a good looking guy; it was because he'd rescued her. That's all it was.

Yeah, believe that and you'll believe anything.

Tom stared back at her and heat flushed Lucy's cheeks. She bit her lip and his eyes dropped to her mouth.

'So we're both pleased we met each other,' he said briskly and stood. 'What would you like to eat? I usually take my main meal in the evening.'

'Just some bread and cheese would be fine,' Lucy said.

'I thought we might go over to see my father this afternoon. He wasn't at the factory. Apparently he's suffering from gout and is at the house. I thought it would be best because my help comes in this afternoon, and she'll prepare dinner for us.'

'Um, and you'll tell your father we're married?'

'I think we're best to get there quickly now that Isabelle barged in on you. She will be telling all and sundry around St Austell. She is a wicked gossip, and now that this affects her, there will be no stopping her. I'm sorry.'

'No, I'm sorry. I probably shouldn't have said anything but she really pressed my buttons.'

Tom flashed that sexy smile at her, and Lucy was pleased she was sitting at the table because her legs went to jelly.

'You'll have to explain that one to me too,' he said.

'She made me angry,' she explained.

'I'll hold your hand when we are with my father, and if you say anything strange like that, I'll squeeze your hand. Hard.'

'I shall be on my best behaviour,' she said demurely.

Tom chuckled and their eyes met and held again. They both looked away and Lucy knew she was in trouble.

Oh, shit.

Three and a bit weeks to get through and not be tempted by her attraction to this sweet man.

Chapter Nineteen

St Austell, Cornwall - 1851

Charles Adams, Tom's father, was a true gentleman. Although obviously taken aback by the news of his son's sudden "marriage", he was unfailingly polite and despite his swollen foot, he stood and crossed the room and took Lucy's hand from Tom, and raised it to his lips.

'Welcome to the family, my dear.' He glanced at Tom, and then his pointed glance to her waistline brought a blush to her face. 'I hope my son hasn't rushed you into this marriage. What did your family say?'

Tom took Lucy's hand as soon as his father had sat in his chair again.

'Um, they are pleased. They live abroad and I wrote them, and they have replied.' Lucy focused on speaking clearly and not contracting her words. 'Yes, they are pleased. Very pleased.'

'Excellent.' Charles turned to Thomas with a wide smile. Lucy had already decided that Thomas took after his father. Despite being a man of wealth with wide business interests, from what Tom had told her as they had walked through town to the harbourside manor, Lucy could see his father was a kind man.

'As soon as your mother comes home we will have a dinner to celebrate, Thomas.'

'That would be excellent, Father,' Tom said. He held Lucy's hand tightly, and she moved a little closer to him. 'I'm looking forward to telling you of my experiences at the Exhibition, Father, but I shall return when you are feeling better. The journey from Plymouth was tiring for Lucy, and I think you need to rest too.' He looked from his father to Lucy. 'Both of you, that is.'

'Your mother will be very pleased to hear your news. I shall send a letter to her today, and I guarantee she will be home by the end of the week.'

'Oh, please tell her not to cut her journey short,' Lucy rushed in.

Charles smiled and shook his head. 'My dear, Margaret will be home in a flash. She will be keen to meet her first daughter-in-law.' He grimaced and used both hands to lift his leg onto the small tapestry stool in front of him. 'Blasted gout. I apologise for my state of health, Lucy. This is a rare occurrence for me, and one that I am not patient with.'

'Perhaps I can help over at the factory tomorrow, Father?' Tom asked with a frown.

Charles waved his hand dismissively. 'Thank you, Tom, but Jacob is doing a fine job.'

'Very well. We shall look forward to visiting again when Mother returns home.' The pressure of Tom's fingers on her arm had increased slightly, and Lucy could sense his unhappiness. 'I'll take Lucy home, and work on the designs that I began in London.'

'Excellent. I look forward to seeing them.'

Lucy was confused; she could sense Tom's agitation, but she could see no reason for it. His father was a good man, who seemed interested in his ideas.

'Come, Lucy. I will take you along the clifftop on the walk back home, and show you more of the area.'

Lucy moved away from Tom's hold and walked across to the chair where Charles sat. 'It's been a pleasure to meet you, sir,' she said simply, and meant it.

'Aye, and you too, lass.' For a moment, his cultured voice took on a rough brogue. 'Thomas has chosen well. I can tell. And I am pleased.'

Lucy lowered her eyes as a warm flush ran up her neck. She could almost believe this was true, that she had married Tom and was going to be a part of this family.

How strange.

She bit down on the side of her cheek, trying to return to reality.

'Get away with the pair of you. You will be busy enough soon, Thomas. Spend some time with your lovely bride.' Charles winked, and the heat moved up to Lucy's cheeks. 'Goodness knows, when your mother returns, she'll have the poor lass at soirees every day.'

Horror filled Lucy; she couldn't think of anything worse.

'We will see you soon, Father.'

Lucy was surprised, and strangely touched when Tom walked across to stand with her and placed an affectionate hand on his father's shoulder.

'You take care. If you need anything, don't hesitate to send us a message.' He took Lucy's hand again and tugged gently.

***

Tom had been very pleased with his father's kindness to Lucy, plus Father had seemed interested in the sights that he had seen in London. Maybe there was a chance that he could move into the design side of their business. He knew he should be less sensitive and more patient with Father, but he was always so slow making decisions.

Tom opened the door and stepped back, letting Lucy precede him onto the path that led through the front garden to the gate. On the way to the harbour, they had walked into town, and down the High Street; he was going to show her the cliff path and their cove on the way home. For a moment, regret filled Tom; it would have been good if this situation was real. His interest in, and his regard for Lucy, was growing each time he saw her, and even holding her hand gave him pleasure.

Her eyes were wide as they walked through the side garden to the gate that led to the cliff path. Hollyhocks grew in profusion along the sun-warmed brick wall, and a riot of nodding pansies edged the garden. The sweet smell of honeysuckle pervaded the air, and the buzzing of the bees crossed the lawn from the small orchard where the apple trees were in bud.

Lucy drew a deep breath and moved closer to him. 'This is so beautiful. It's what I always imagined England to be like.'

He shook his head with a smile 'This is not England, Lucy. This is Cornwall.'

'Well, it's still beautiful.'

'I'm pleased you approve. It will make your time here more pleasant if you like your surroundings.'

'Oh, I do. It's fabulous.'

'Fabulous?' he asked with a frown. 'But it is real.'

Lucy frowned. 'Another word I'm using incorrectly? I'll have to be careful if I do have to go to these "soirees" your father mentioned. Fabulous, to me, means amazing, beautiful, wonderful.'

Tom nodded. 'I can see that. To me, it means something mythical. Your language fascinates me. It appears we have the same words, but the meaning has changed.'

'And that is another good reason for me to keep a low profile. Just stay in your home, and walk with you occasionally. That is, if you want to and if you have the time. I don't want to be a burden. I owe you so much already.'

'True. If Mother spends too much time with you, you'll have to pretend you've lost your voice, so you don't use the wrong words.'

'God, that scares me. Soirees! No, thank you. I'm not even social back home.' Lucy stared past him, and Tom picked up on her unhappiness. 'You know, if it wasn't for Joshua, I think I could stay here quite happily.'

'What would you miss? Apart from your little boy, I mean.'

She looked up at him as they reached the gate, and the sheen of moisture in Lucy's eyes surprised him and made him sad.

'To be honest?' she said slowly. ' My little boy, but nothing else. Certainly not our life.'

'Perhaps when you go back, you will have to make some changes?'

'Thank you,' she said stepping through the gate.

'For?'

'For being so sure I will go back. I try not to worry about it. But you are right, when—not if— I go home, there'll be many changes. The way I had been living at home wasn't satisfactory, and not good for Joshua to just be the two of us all the time. I never went out very much. I lost most of my friends when I met Royden.'

'I'm sorry to see you sad. Come.' Tom crooked his elbow, and his arm tingled when Lucy put her arm through his. 'I'll take you for a walk and tell you some rollicking tales of my childhood here. Tales to curdle your blood and make you smile.'

Her giggle made him smile. 'Rollicking?'

'Yes, you are about to see Smuggler's Cove, the site of many bloodthirsty battles when John and Jacob and I were growing up.'

'It sounds like fun. That's the sort of happy childhood I would like to give to Joshua. Brothers and sisters to play with, but that won't be happening.'

Tom's face warmed. He didn't like to ask why, but his expression must have revealed his thoughts.

'May I tell you why? Or would you prefer not to know?' Lucy's voice was quiet as they walked along the clifftop.

'If you are happy to tell me, I will be pleased to listen. I think we have struck up a good . . . friendship, already, Lucy. You have shown that you trust me.'

'Oh, I do, Tom. You don't know how much I appreciate what you've done to help me. I just don't want to burden you with my problems.'

'I'm happy to listen if it helps.'

Lucy remained quiet and didn't answer as they walked along the clifftop. The early mist had cleared, and the clear pale blue sky above was host to a flock of seabirds wheeling and calling raucously above them. They reached the curve in the path that looked over the cove where he had played with his brothers and their friends from the village. Tom looked to the west and marvelled at how much the area had grown since his father had expanded the family pottery business. It was no longer a village; in fact, several of the villages had joined to form the sprawling township of St Austell. He stopped walking and Lucy removed her arm from his. She stood quietly, close beside him, looking over the sea, her arms folded. Close enough that he could feel the tension in her, but he didn't speak again. He would wait until she spoke.

A couple of fishing boats were moored at the base of the cliff, and Tom watched as the nets were hauled in. Finally, Lucy broke the silence.

'I was taken in by Royden's determination to make me want him. He was persistent, and he persevered with flowers, gifts, and fancy restaurants until I gave in. I didn't understand why he wanted me so badly then, but now I think it was simply the thrill of the chase. Whatever he wants, he's always had. I think I was a challenge to him; I was one of the few women who didn't fawn over him and fall at his feet.' She smiled. 'Not literally, that is. By the time I woke up to what he was really like, it was too late. I was pregnant. I'm sorry to say he is not a very nice person.'

'You didn't marry?' he asked quietly.

Lucy shook her head and turned to look at him finally. Twin spots of colour stained her cheeks a rosy pink. Her eyes were clear now and she regarded him steadily.

'No, I was already pregnant with Joshua. We've never married.'

'You were having his child and he *refused* to marry you?'

'No. *I* refused to marry him. Oh, he tried hard enough to do the "right" thing. It would have looked better for him, you see. To keep up appearances. If he was going to be a father, it would have been better for him if we'd been married.'

'And you didn't think so?'

'No. He did his dash very early on. I will never forget what Royden said to me when I told him I was pregnant.' Lucy stared at him and lifted her chin. 'He demanded to know whether it was his child, and then when I assured him it was, he told me in no uncertain terms to—the exact term he used was—"to get rid of it".'

Tom was horrified. He lifted his hand to reach out to her, but before he could speak, Lucy kept talking. 'He accused me of getting pregnant to trap him. Remember, this is the man who wouldn't give up on me. He'd got what he wanted, the thrill of the chase was over, and the last thing he wanted was a child. He conveniently forgot all that, and it quickly became my fault.'

'So you moved away to England to live with your aunt.'

She shook her head. 'No, I stayed with him for over three years. I figured that he might come around and at least Joshua would have a home and a father. We lived together, and things went along okay, although I was lonely. Until a month ago when I found out I was kidding myself. Royden is a—I'm sure you'll know the term—philanderer. I should never have moved in with him. He's never been one bit interested in Joshua, and the final straw was when I discovered he's been seeing another woman.'

Tom drew in his breath. 'He sounds like an absolute cad.'

Lucy's smile was bitter. 'That's the perfect term for him. But he is the father of my sweet little boy. And I have to remember that.'

Tom reached out and took her hands in his; hands that were as cold as ice. Lucy took a step towards him and looked down at her feet. She sniffed and as he watched, a tear spilled over onto her cheek.

He let go of her hands and held his arms open. She stepped into them, and rested her head on his shoulder, her hands slipping around his waist.

'I don't know what to do, Tom. When I go back. If I even get back.' Her voice shook.

'You will. I do not doubt that.' He rested his head on her sweet-smelling hair and closed his eyes. Having Lucy in his arms was wonderful; he wished he could help her. It was going to be very hard to do what he must, no matter how right holding her in his arms was. He had to resist her charm and his feelings.

After holding her close for a long moment, she relaxed in his arms and Tom spoke quietly. 'I don't know how to help you, but I do wish I could. Very much so. If I'm honest, it will only confuse you even more.' He took a deep breath and lifted his head. 'I don't know why, Lucy and I don't how, but I do believe I was meant to meet you at the stones the other afternoon. I believe that we were meant to meet. Maybe it was so I could help you get back. Or look after you while you are here.'

Lucy leaned back slightly and looked up at him. Her eyes were clear and her expression was calmer than it had been. 'I know exactly what you're saying. Aunt Alice told me about it. It's such an unknown to me, and maybe to you, this whole travel thing. But we have no choice but to believe in it. You called them fairy paths, my aunt called them threads. She travelled too, and she met a man, a long time before her time. I heard the expression she used, it was so beautiful it stayed with me.'

'What did she call it?'

'The threads that bind, and she said it is those threads that pull you to where you are supposed to be. To your destiny.' Her beautiful eyes were intent on his. 'How can it be my destiny, Tom? I have a child in my time. I can't stay here no matter how much I—'

'No matter how much you?'

'No matter how much I want to stay here with you,' she whispered. 'I've only known you for a few days, but it's as though I've known you all my life. I feel different when you're with me. I've never felt like this before. Even when Joshua was born. It's the strangest feeling. Do you feel it too? Is that what you meant when you said you couldn't be honest?'

The hope in her voice brought Tom undone. Her eyes widened as he let go of her fingers and lifted both hands to gently cup her cheeks. For the love of God, he couldn't help himself. Her lips were pink and rosy and parted softly as she let out a gentle sigh.

He groaned. 'I'm not very good at this, but all I know is that I've wanted to do it since you stumbled through those stones. I don't know how I'm going to let you go, Lucy.'

Tom leaned down and gently brushed his lips across hers.

Chapter Twenty

Violet Cottage, March - 2019

Beth's brow furrowed in a frown and she stared at the screen. 'I've found him, Mum.'

'What do you mean you've found him?' Lucy had been sitting enjoying the early spring sunshine as her daughter's fingers flew over the buttons on the phone. Occasionally Beth would sigh, peer at the screen and then shake her head.

'Thomas Egbert Adams was born in St Austell on the 17th October 1827.' She grinned triumphantly. 'Does that sound right?'

Lucy put her hand to her mouth, as the blood seemed to drain from her head. 'Where? What . . . how . . I mean how did you find that?'

'I joined ancestry.com. You owe me seventy pounds.'

Lucy could barely speak as her head spun. For a moment, she thought the sun had gone behind a cloud and then realised she was feeling faint. She put her hands over her face and covered her eyes until her head stopped spinning. When she finally lifted her hands away, Beth was still intent on her phone.

'You got all that information from looking on your phone?'

'Yes. I *told* you there would be something there, Mum. And if you were more techno-savvy, you could have found that out ages ago.'

Lucy cleared her throat. 'What else is there. Is the date he . . .' She couldn't bring herself to say it. If Tom was dead, would he still be alive if she managed to go back? If he was, would he still be young, or would she be able to go back to the time when he would be twenty-six years older too? She closed her eyes again. There was so much unknown. That would make him fifty-three. Alice had assured her that if she followed the instructions and picked the time, the time would have passed for him too. 'The threads that bind, love,' she used to say. 'Time will ensure that you go where you must.' Even after Lucy had travelled, Alice's words had been cryptic, but with what Alice—and Thelma, back in 1851— had taught her about the process, Lucy had faith she could do it.

Unless Tom hadn't lived that long, in which case she had left going back too late. She put her head in her hands again. 'I need to know if he is alive.' Her voice was muffled.

'Mum.' Beth's hand was gentle on hers. 'There's no date of death in the ancestry record. It's blank.'

'Why not? What does that mean?'

Beth's hand moved against Lucy's as she shrugged. 'I don't know. Maybe he'd moved away from the parish where his birth is recorded. But there is no record of his death in the St Austell parish. Let me keep searching.'

'Is there . . . is there anything else? Is there a marriage record?' The thought of Tom marrying Isabelle after she had left had haunted Lucy for years, and she had to keep reminding herself that she had chosen to stay with Royden. She sat straight as she realised what she was putting Beth through. Tom was her *father*, for God's sake. She grabbed her daughter's hand. 'I'm so sorry, Bethie. I didn't even think about how you would be feeling about all this.'

'It's okay. I'm fine. I've had time to get my head around it all since you told me. I want to find out as much as I can about him so I know him too.' She held the phone up. 'Look, there are a lot more hits here. Come on, we'll go inside and boot up my laptop. I'll hotspot it to my phone. It'll be easier to read together. If you're going travelling back to him, *I* want to know what you're going to find before you go. I'll feel a little easier about it.'

Lucy managed to steady her hands enough to make a pot of tea while Beth set up her laptop.

She carried the tray from the kitchen to the small table in the dining alcove.

'Have you hotwired it?' she asked.

Beth grinned up at her. 'Yes, Mum I have hot *spotted* my laptop to my phone. We're right to go. Are you okay?'

Lucy nodded. 'I am. Just a bit nervous. I think it might be easier going through the stones not knowing what I was going to find.'

Beth bit her lip. 'Maybe you won't have to go. I'll worry about you, Mum. I'll want to know that you're okay.'

'Now you know what it's like to worry. When I heard where you and Silas had been—' She shook her head. Lucy's hand shook again as she poured the tea into two fine teacups. 'I need to pull myself together,' she muttered.

Beth smiled 'What is it about being here that makes me drink tea? I've hardly drunk any coffee since I arrived.'

'Alice's legacy. She was an advocate for a cup of tea solving the ills of the world.'

'I remember how much I enjoyed her company when we were over here when I was little. I wish I'd known her better.'

'She loved you and Josh. Even though she hardly saw you, she was always interested in what you were doing.'

'That was Dad's—I mean Royden's—doing, wasn't it? I know he hated you talking about her and he always disappeared when you were reading her letters when we were kids.'

Lucy held back a sigh. 'Water under the bridge now.'

'Mum?' Beth bit her lip again and frowned.

'Yes, love, what's wrong?'

'I just want to tell you something.'

'What is it?'

'After meeting Silas, and knowing what it's like to love, I want you to know that I appreciate so much more the sacrifice you made by staying with Royden, so I'd have a father and a secure upbringing. Now that you've left him, you're so much happier. And I guess, I have to accept that if you do find Tom, you'll be completely happy. I understand now.'

'Oh, Beth. Some of the years were okay. I should have been stronger, but I couldn't justify leaving. But once you and Josh left home I—'

'You woke up and realised that he'd been playing around for years.'

Lucy widened her eyes. 'You knew?'

'Mum. *Everyone* knew. But you seemed happy enough in your own world. With your job and your friends. Josh and I often talked about what we should say, but we both assumed that you knew and that you were putting up with him.'

'It's the biggest regret of my life that I ignored what was going on for so long. I guess I knew deep down, but Royden is Joshua's father, and he provided for you and made sure you had everything you wanted and paid for your education.'

'Did he know? About me?'

'That he wasn't your father? Yes, I was honest. I told him when I came back. He was waiting here in this cottage the day I came back through the stones. I'll never forget that day as long as I live.'

Beth's eyes widened and she drew in a breath. 'I want you to tell me all about what happened, but first have a look at this.' She clicked her mouse and a company logo filled the screen, and a series of images rolled across the top of the screen.

'St Austell. Today and some historical photos. Apparently, there's a pottery museum there now, all about the china clay industry in the nineteenth century.'

'Look!' Lucy said as her excitement built. 'That's Smugglers Cove. I've stood on the top of that cliff. It's where your father kissed me the first time.' She looked at Lucy. 'Where I fell in love with your father. And I've never loved another man since.'

Chapter Twenty-One

St Austell - 1851

Lucy widened her eyes as the pale sunlight shadowed her face. Surprise and elation flooded through her when Tom's lips touched hers. The emotion that gripped her was so sudden and unexpected, her cheeks burned. Sensation after sensation flooded through her as she was swept into the moment; her hands went around his neck and she clung to him as his mouth touched hers again. Softness, warmth and happiness fought for precedence.

The pressure increased and Lucy opened her mouth as Tom gently explored with his warm lips. Tingles ran down her legs, and her hands shook as she held him close.

'I don't want to leave you either, but I must,' she murmured against his mouth. 'Eventually. But we have over three weeks to be together until I have to leave. For those weeks, I am yours. I've only known you for a matter of days, but I can't imagine not being with you, Tom. It's hard to understand, but that's how I feel.'

He pulled back a little and looked down at her. 'Are you sure, Lucy? Are you really sure?'

'I've never been more certain of anything in my entire life,' she said. 'I can't understand it. I can't explain it, and I'm not going to try. I just want to be in this moment—these moments, these days, these weeks—with you. For the time we have. Until I go back to my real life.'

His arms went around her again, and Tom rested his cheek against hers. 'We shall make this our real life for the next month.' He took her hand in his and his eyes were full of meaning as they stayed on hers. 'Shall we go home?'

Heat burned Lucy's cheeks and she looked down shyly. 'Yes. I would like that very much.'

***

March - 2019

'Look, Mum. The business at St Austell went from strength to strength. After you left. Look at this. This site, there's a lot of information and images.'

'Of Tom?'

'No. of the area. The mountains.'

Lucy leaned over and read the screen that Beth was pointing to. 'That's not the same place. There were no mountains there. Just a small hill behind his cottage.'

'Read it, Mum. This historical site says "any visitor to St Austell is likely to be impressed by the Cornish Alps, a manmade structure which dominates the surrounding landscape and represents the story of china clay. They were formed as every ton of usable china clay that was mined brought with it five tonnes of waste."'

'I guess that's why I didn't see them. They weren't formed back then.'

Beth kept reading the screen, but Lucy was scanning for photographs. For images. Anything of Tom.

'Railways and tramways were built to transport the material to the coast. By 1910, Cornwall was producing some fifty per cent of the world's china clay, something in the region of one million tonnes every year. The business was started by Charles Adams in 1846, and by 1860, 65,000 tonnes of china clay were being mined in the St Austell area every year by twelve thousand workers. Small villages quickly grew to cater for the industry. West Polmear, for example, which had a pre-china clay population of nine, was thoroughly transformed by Charles Adams, who invested huge sums of money building a safe harbour for ships, and houses and factories for workers. Adams built a manor overlooking the harbour which is now a museum displaying the development of the china clay industry.'

Lucy put a hand to her mouth. 'That's where I met Tom's father. At the house above the harbour. I hope I can find it when I'm there.'

'We can Google Map it,' Beth said. 'I assume it won't have moved.'

Lucy couldn't help the chuckle that bubbled up from her chest. 'Oh, Beth, you are so clever. I have no idea what that means, but I love it.'

Beth reached over and kissed her cheek. 'You won't need to understand it where you're going.'

'Your grandfather, Charles Adams, and his wife, Margaret, lived in a manor overlooking the harbour.' Tears misted her eyes, and she blinked them away. 'They were such lovely people and made me so welcome in the short time I was there. It will be so sad if I go there now; they'd be long gone. The sad thing is they never knew that Tom had a daughter. I hope John and Jacob gave them grandchildren,' she said quietly. 'They made me so welcome, I felt guilty leaving without them knowing why. I couldn't say goodbye. Tom and I just left. It's so hard to believe the house where there were such happy times is a museum now. I spent a few interesting and really enjoyable afternoons there.' Lucy looked closely at Beth. 'You know, I've always seen your father in your eyes, but as you've grown up, I can see Margaret. I hadn't ever thought of that before.'

'I'd love to go back with you, Mum. Please?'

'Not this time, Beth.' Lucy stared at the clock on the wall and watched the large hand tick around as she thought. 'Maybe, just maybe another time and I'm not promising anything. If it all works out, I'll come back and tell you. And maybe you could visit with me then. But like I said, no promises.'

Beth's eyes misted. 'I'll accept that. Thank you, Mum.' She cleared her throat and pointed to the screen. 'Look at this, Mum. Keep reading.'

Lucy followed Beth's finger as it trailed down the screen.

Tom's name jumped out at her.

'Charles Adams' youngest son, Thomas, was a well-respected designer at the factory, and the white porcelain products from the business at St Austell to this day still grace the best dining rooms in the counties, as well as being exported to Europe. Thomas Adams moved to Copenhagen and gained fame as one of Europe's top porcelain designers in the latter half of the nineteenth century.'

'Copenhagen,' Lucy said slowly. 'Did he ever go back to Cornwall? Maybe he spent the rest of his life in Scandinavia, and that's why there's no record of his—'

'I wonder if that's where—' Beth's face was stricken as she looked at her. 'I'm sorry, Mum. This isn't helping, is it?'

'You wonder if that's where his life ended,' Lucy said sadly. 'I guess I'll find out when I go back.'

Chapter Twenty-Two

St Austell - 1851

Tom pushed open the door of the cottage and Lucy laughed as he lifted her into his arms.

'What are you doing?'

'You might think I'm mad, but I want to carry you over the threshold again. Will you be my wife for the time you are here, dearest Lucy?'

Love for this man flooded through Lucy as Tom smiled down at her. 'I will.' She smiled back. 'Or should I say, I do?'

Tom kept her in his arms as he carefully navigated the narrow staircase. His eyes burned into hers, and Lucy trembled with anticipation until she wondered if she'd be able to stand on her shaking legs when he put her down. Tom went to the room across the small landing from hers and pushed the door open with his foot.

'This is where I usually sleep.'

'And you moved to that tiny room downstairs to give me privacy?' Lucy had peeked into the room where he was sleeping and it was the size of a cupboard.

Tom didn't answer as he gently lowered her to her feet. His hands were warm on her waist and Lucy arched her head back as his lips trailed down her neck. His lips and his fingers sent exquisite feelings shooting through every nerve ending in her body. She'd never felt that way before. Royden flashed briefly into her thoughts, but she closed her mind to that and gave herself up to Tom's hands and mouth as he slowly undid the small pearl buttons on her blouse, and then slipped it over her shoulders. He smiled and raised his eyebrows as he looked at her white lace twentieth-century bra.

'Now that looks like a challenge.' The huskiness of his voice touched her, knowing that he was feeling as much as she was.

Lucy pressed her lips onto his, reached around her back and undid the clip. Her small breasts were exposed as the bra joined her blouse on the floor.

She was barely aware of the rest of her clothing, and then Tom's, following it.

***

'I've been thinking,' Tom said one afternoon in his bed a few days later, as Lucy's head rested on his shoulder. She had moved into his room on the top floor, and as well as spending the nights there, they often adjourned there through the day for some very pleasant interludes. They had left his house only once in the past three days when Lucy wanted to see the sunrise over the sea one morning.

She rolled over and stared at him, before trailing her fingers down his bare chest. 'That sounds like a dangerous activity. I can think of a much nicer way to spend the afternoon in your bed.'

A slow smile spread across her face when Tom chuckled. 'Ah, I love me a wanton wench.' There was no conversation for a while as she was thoroughly kissed.

Lucy rolled away, propped her head on one hand and smiled down at him. 'So what have you been thinking about? It's about time we thought about eating.'

'I've been thinking about coming with you.'

'To your mother's soiree tomorrow?' They had received a message this morning that Margaret had returned home and was looking forward to meeting Thomas's wife. He knew Lucy was already het up about going there by herself. 'That would be good. I'm really nervous about meeting the ladies from the town.'

Tom shook his head. 'God, no. That would be totally inappropriate. I'll take you there but I'm not invited to the afternoon tea. I didn't mean there.'

Lucy frowned. 'Where to?' Her expression changed as he stared at her, as she understood what he was saying. 'No, Tom. It would be too risky. It's bad enough that I have to go through the stones. No, I don't mean bad as in going home.' Her words tumbled over one another. 'I mean I want to go home to Joshua, but I also don't want to leave you. But it's all such an unknown. We don't know the risks involved until we go back to the cottage and talk to Thelma.'

'I know you have to go.' Tom chose his words carefully. 'Don't think for one moment that I don't understand that. I know you have a child waiting for you. But I don't want to lose you, Lucy. I don't think I can bear it.' He reached up and pulled her down to him so that her head rested on his shoulder again. Her hot tears warmed his skin. 'If it means leaving here and everything familiar to me, so be it. I would choose you over my life here.'

Tears filled Lucy's eyes as she stared at him, He reached and wiped them away. 'I love you, Lucy. You are part of me. You are in my blood, my soul, my life.'

'I know. It was our destiny. But we can't play with time. Who knows what would happen?'

'But you're here. You came through.'

'But it was an accident. I told you. I was with Joshua, and I tripped and put my hand out.'

'Your aunt has travelled, and more than once.'

'I know. I mean, I don't know.'

'Does that mean you don't want me to come back with you?'

'No, it doesn't but also, yes, it does. I don't want you to come to any harm.' Lucy rolled over and sat on the side of the bed, her back to him. She leaned forward and put her hands over her face. 'Can we not talk about this until we go back to Glastonbury? We'll see what Thelma says.' Her voice was muffled, and regret lodged in Tom's throat. He hadn't meant to upset her.

'I'm sorry, Lucy. I shouldn't have brought it up.' Tom slid his legs over the sides of the high bed and walked around to sit beside her. Her face was streaked with tears and his heart broke. 'I'm sorry, my love. Stop worrying, and don't cry anymore. We will work it out.'

She nodded and he reached over and tucked her loose hair behind her ear. 'Let's go eat, and then we're going for a walk.'

Her eyes brightened a little. He had noticed how much she'd loved being on the cliffs overlooking the cove. 'Where to?'

'To make it easier for you, I thought it would be best if we went over to visit my mother before the soiree tomorrow when you'll have a flock of chattering women to contend with. As soon as Mother meets you, she will love you.'

He grinned when Lucy cocked one eyebrow and her lips tilted in a smile.

'Do you think so? The woman who stole her son's heart while he was away from his home.'

'I know so. I know she will love you, and I know you will get along just fine.'

'Hmm. We will see.'

Chapter Twenty-Three

St Austell, Cornwall - 1851

Before they left Lucy insisted on taking a bath in the hip bath in the small washroom at the back of the house. Tom shook his head as he tipped the warm water over her.

'It's a wonder you have any skin left you wash it so much.'

'It's what we do. It's hot in Australia and I shower twice a day at home.'

'Interesting habits.'

'Clean habits,' Lucy said with a laugh and threw the flannel at him. 'I'd heard about the Pommie's Saturday being bath day.'

'It's a nice habit you've introduced me to.'

Lucy had been interested to see Thomas washing every day with a sponge soaked in cool water and vinegar.

'One worth keeping,' Lucy said as she dipped her hair in the warm water.

Tom was waiting with the rectangle of white flat woven cloth. It bore very little resemblance to a towel for Lucy, but she'd managed to dry herself on one over the past few days.

She dressed carefully and bound her wet hair in a tight French roll. 'Does it make me look older?' she asked. 'More serious? Do I look the part?'

'You look beautiful. And please stop worrying. Meeting my father was painless, wasn't it? And meeting Mother will be even easier. Trust me, she is kind and caring, and will accept you just as you are.'

'Just as I am? So I don't look right?' Lucy widened her eyes.

Tom put his hands on her shoulders. 'You look just right. Now, take a deep breath, and think about your voice and your words. Just be careful.'

'Okay. I'll be as quiet as a church mouse. She can think I'm shy.'

As Tom turned to the door he put his head back and laughed. 'That, my dear, is one thing you are not.'

Lucy pulled a face at him as she took his arm and they headed to the cliff path.

##

I was right, Tom thought as he sat with his father in the parlour at the harbour house. Laughter came from the garden where Mother was showing Lucy her prize flowers. There had been no shyness, and certainly no quiet since his mother and his "wife" had met an hour ago. They had taken afternoon tea—Tom was starving and had appreciated the sandwiches and cakes that Mrs Pitkin, the cook, had produced when they had arrived just after three o'clock. They had lingered on the clifftop on the way, and Lucy had listened as Tom had told her more stories of playing pirates and smugglers when he and his brothers had been boys. 'That's the sort of childhood I want for Joshua,' she'd said quietly.

'I could be there and make sure he has one just like it,' Tom replied.

'Tom, please don't.' Lucy had been quiet after that.

'Tell me about the sorts of flowers in your parents' garden,' Mother asked as they came in through the conservatory.

Lucy glanced across at Tom. 'I don't know their names. I just enjoy the colour and the perfume. It's a much hotter climate where they live—I mean where I came from, and we don't have the soft pretty flowers that you have here.'

'Why did you leave home and come to England?'

'I came over to care for my aunt. She lives in a cottage at Glastonbury. She has a beautiful garden that you would enjoy too, but nowhere near as big as your grounds.'

'Margaret wears herself out in the garden. She prefers to be in charge much to the gardener's displeasure,' Charles said. 'Now enough of this tea and garden chatter. I think it's well past time that we had a drink to celebrate your marriage.'

'That's an excellent idea, Charles. I will tell Cook that you will stay for dinner. Is that suitable to you, Lucy, or have you planned dinner at the house?' His mother's smile hadn't left her face since they had arrived, and as usual, she didn't stay still for very long.

'I'm not sure what Mrs Hepple will leave for us.' Lucy glanced over at him, and Tom raised his eyebrow. He was pleased when she gave a tiny nod.

'If it suits Tom, that would be very nice. Thank you.'

'I'm so pleased.' His mother hurried across to the carved wine cabinet and took out four glasses, and then placed them on a tray with a bottle of sherry.

'Margaret, please sit down. I am not an invalid,' Father snapped. He flicked a glance to

Lucy. 'I am sorry for sounding like a grumpy old man, my dear, but my wife thinks that a case of gout has incapacitated me.'

His mother bestowed a sweet smile on his father. 'Be careful, my dear, or you will find water in your sherry glass.'

Tom took pity on Lucy as she looked from one to the other.

'Don't worry, Lucy. That is how my loving parents talk to each other all the time.'

She smiled and looked relieved.

Tom reached over and took over the bottle. 'Sit down, Mother, before you get into trouble again.'

She laughed and sat beside Lucy. 'Oh my dear, you do not know how I have longed for this moment. Over thirty years of marriage, three rambunctious sons, and now I finally have the daughter I always longed for. And such a beautiful girl, isn't she, Charles?' Margaret picked up Lucy's hand and squeezed it.

Tom's heart clenched as Lucy smiled and his mother wiped a tear from the corner of her eye. He poured the sherry into the delicate glasses and passed them across to his mother and Lucy, before sitting near his father and placing the other two glasses on the table between them.

Charles held up his glass and smiled at them. 'To Thomas and Lucy. Congratulations on your marriage and welcome to the family.'

***

Dinner was a light-hearted affair, and Lucy had relaxed and enjoyed the evening. The word had spread and Tom's older brother, Jacob, had arrived as they sat in the conservatory after dinner. Like the rest of the family, he seemed to be pleasant and kind-hearted and welcomed her warmly to the family.

The rest of the week passed in a similar fashion. The afternoon tea with the ladies of the town passed pleasantly, and Lucy managed not to get herself into any difficult conversations. She was vague about her family and managed to change the subject a couple of times without it being obvious. Margaret kept a close eye on her and made sure that she was introduced to every woman who attended, most of whom were married to men who worked at the pottery works. She was invited to an embroidery circle, two afternoon walks and three afternoon teas, but Margaret hovered and intervened on her behalf.

'Ladies, ladies. Dear Lucy will have plenty of time ahead to join in our social activities. Thomas has taken a few weeks off from the works, and they are spending their honeymoon at home.'

'That seems very strange.' A familiar voice came from behind Lucy, and before she turned, she knew it was Isabelle Lyndhurst. She was pleased when Margaret stepped between them.

'Oh hello, Isabelle. I wasn't aware you were attending today.'

Isabelle's eyebrows arched. 'Oh, I wouldn't have missed it for the world, even though I am not in a mood for being social. I apologise for my tardiness'—her glittering dark eyes ran up and down Lucy's plain skirt and blouse—'but as you will understand I have been quite unwell this week. Mother says it is the shock.'

Lucy stepped forward and kept her voice flat and quiet. 'It is nice to see you again. I am very pleased you made the *effort* to attend.'

Nice was the blandest word she could think of. *God, that Isabelle was a cow.* If nothing else came out of her visit here, at least she'd saved Tom from a life of misery.

Margaret took her arm and led her over to a group of older ladies who were twittering in the corner.

'Lucy, these are the ladies who are organising the charity bazaar . . .'

By the time the women had introduced themselves, there was no sign of Isabelle, and Lucy suspected that Margaret had asked her to leave, although it was never mentioned.

The next week, Tom had a meeting at the pottery works. Lucy spent a pleasant afternoon up at the harbour house with Margaret, before returning home to the routine she had established. The ease with which she had settled into the lifestyle of this time surprised her, and if not for Joshua waiting for her at the cottage, she could have stayed longer. Although she knew that would be dangerous. She was falling deeper into love with Tom every day, and the thought of leaving him terrified her as much as the thought of not getting back to Joshua. Life was surprisingly busy—she appreciated what she took for granted at home—but Lucy ensured that she spent an hour each day, in a quiet time, thinking about her little boy, and keeping the image of his dear little face, and his voice, in her thoughts.

As far as Tom coming back with her, she knew in her heart it wasn't right for him. His family was here, his work was here, and she knew he had been satisfied with his life before she had stumbled into it.

It wouldn't be the right choice for him. No matter how much Tom loved her, and no matter how much he pleaded.

Chapter Twenty-Four

St Austell, Cornwall - 1851

It was hard for Lucy to believe that she had been in Cornwall for only three weeks. Sometimes it seemed much longer, especially when she thought of Joshua. Her memory was fading and that frightened her. She could see his little face in her mind, and hear his voice and his cute words, but she had trouble holding the memory of feeling him against her. Of his sweet smell after he was bathed, and his soft downy hair against her cheek as she rocked him to sleep.

'Mumma.' His little voice drifted in her thoughts as she sat beside Tom in the train on the way to Glastonbury. They had decided not to tell Charles and Margaret that they were leaving. Tom said he would decide what to say when he returned. He had finally accepted that Lucy was right and he must stay here. They were both tense and sat stiffly in the noisy carriage with very little conversation.

Last night had been bittersweet, both knowing it was their last night together in the house that had become a home to Lucy over the past three weeks.

'I'm torn, Tom.' She had clung to him in the early hours. 'I must go back. I want to go back to my little boy. But I want to stay here with you equally as much.'

Tom's voice broke as he put his lips to her forehead. 'I know, sweetheart. I know you can't choose, and I wouldn't expect you to.'

'Maybe I could come back in a year or two. I could bring Joshua. We could say that he was born while I was back visiting my parents,'

'No, that would be a lie and it would not be fair to his father.'

Lucy had turned from Tom and curled into a tight ball. Sobs wracked her body, and her heart felt as though it was being squeezed out of her chest. The other side of the bed dipped and all was quiet.

She squeezed her eyes shut, trying to stop the tears.

Think of Joshua, she told herself. *He will be missing me. Think of the joy of holding him again.*

Think of Tom, her heart told her. You love him.

She opened her eyes as a gentle hand touched her shoulder.

'Lucy?' Tom sat beside her and she pushed her hair back from her face so she could look at him. He was holding a cup. 'I want you to drink this so you can get some sleep.'

'What is it?' Her voice was husky from crying.

He smiled his beautiful smile at her and her heart clenched. 'It's my father's best French cognac. I have a few bottles here so Mother doesn't know how many he brought back from Plymouth last week.'

Lucy smiled through her tears. 'I do love your parents. You are very lucky.'

'I am. And they have grown to love you in our short time together. I don't want you to be sad. I have my family, and I will continue with my work.' He handed her the glass and Lucy swallowed the contents in one gulp, spluttering and grabbing her throat as the liquid burned its way down her gut.

'Oh my God. I won't need to sleep. I think you've killed me.' She leaned over and put her head on his shoulder. 'Think of me, Tom. Think of me every day as I will think of you. I will never forget you, and I will do everything I can to come back one day. I promise you that.'

'Every morning, I shall walk to the cliff, or wherever I am, I will go outside and watch the sunrise, and I will send my love to you over the years.'

'And I will wait to feel it.' Lucy's throat had stopped burning, and her eyelids began to droop. 'I think I want to go to sleep now. Will you hold me, please?' She had slept in his arms and he was still holding her close when they woke to embark on their journey that day. They left in the afternoon on the mail train, and travelled through the night, arriving in Glastonbury just after sunrise.

The speed of the train slowed and the conductor walked through the carriage. 'Next stop, Glastonbury,' he announced.

Tom reached down and picked up the one small bag they had brought with them. As soon as they spoke to Thelma—if she had returned from Scotland—Lucy was going to attempt the journey back.

If the time suited.

***

Tom had been mindful of not letting his emotions take hold as they journeyed towards the place where he knew Lucy would leave him. He knew it wouldn't take much for her to break again, so he remained cheery every time she spoke, although that wasn't often. He helped her onto the platform and they stood watching as the train began to move away. As she turned towards him he smiled, and she tipped her head to the side.

'What?'

'I was just thinking how you have transformed into a woman of 1851 with very little effort. You really look as though you belong now, Lucy. Very different to the woman in the strange clothes who stumbled into my arms a month ago.'

'Strangely I do feel as though I belong too.' She reached over and took his hand. 'But that has more to do with you than any clothes or customs. I don't think I made too many mistakes, did I?'

He raised his eyebrows and grinned. 'Ah, I recall a night at the harbour house where the sherry loosened your tongue. Mother and Father intend to travel to Morocco one day to see all the wondrous things you spoke of.'

'Hmm, I think I did slip up a little that night.'

'You did.' Tom was pleased to see Lucy smile too, as she stood on her toes and leaned towards him. He closed his eyes as her lips brushed his cheek.

'I will never forget you, Tom.' Her voice dropped to a whisper. 'You are the love of my life.'

He cleared his throat and spoke before he broke. 'Enough of that. I have a gift for you.' He reached into his pocket and pulled out a small cloth bag and put it in her fingers. 'You don't have to wear it, but I thought it might remind you of me sometimes.'

Her smile was wide. 'I will need no reminding, my love.' She opened the drawstring of the bag and tipped the contents into her hand.

Tom had designed two small white suns from the finest clay. Shards of light joined the two porcelain orbs.

'Oh, it's so beautiful.' She blinked away tears and handed it to him and turned around. 'Please put it on me.'

Tom's fingers shook as he fastened the clasp on the fine gold chain. He leaned down and kissed the soft skin on the side of her neck.

'I will never take it off,' she said softly.

Reaching down he picked up the bag they shared. 'As it is only early, shall we go straight to the cottage and see if your relative has returned before we go and seek lodging for the night?'

One more night. That was all he asked. If Lucy wouldn't let him go back to her time, Tom wanted one more night to remember for the rest of his life.

Until she returned. She had promised, but his certainty of that happening would have to wait until they spoke to the woman in the cottage.

THE THREADS THAT BIND

Chapter Twenty-Five

Violet Cottage -1851

Thelma had returned only three days ago, she told Lucy and Tom when she had ushered them into the cottage after Lucy had explained why they were there. 'Come in, come away in.' She led them into the kitchen and Lucy looked around at the almost familiar cottage.

'So you're not surprised by what I ask? You believe me?' she asked.

'Aye, of course, I do.' Lucy had been surprised by her broad Scottish accent. 'You're not the first, lassie.'

'I'm not?'

'No, but you are the first from the future.'

'So Alice was never here?'

Thelma shook her head. 'Nae, I know of no Alice.' She crossed to the table and sat beside Lucy and Tom. Tom held her hand tightly under the table, and she could feel the tension in his fingers as Thelma took them through the process of reversing her journey.

The smell of the yellow roses growing over the back of the cottage drifted in through the open door.

Lucy's stomach was churning as she looked at Tom in disbelief, and then turned back to Thelma.

'Today? At noon?' Disbelief, hope, regret and sadness, and a little bit of fear, held her in a relentless grip.

'Yes, my dear. You must go at the same time you came through, and you must touch the same stone in the same place as when you travelled here.'

'Are you sure? Have you travelled?'

'I am a McLaren woman.'

'What does that mean?' Tom interrupted.

'It means that I, and Lucy, come from a line of women who can travel much more easily than others.'

'So others can go if they wish?' Tom's fingers squeezed hers as he leaned forward.

'Yes, but it is not as easy.' Thelma replied. 'Not from what I've heard.'

Tom shook his head. 'Who would ever have known that something like this exists?'

'Many people.' Thelma gestured to the field. 'There are similar portals scattered around the country. Many in Scotland and Ireland too.'

'So why would I have ended up here?'

'I think from what I am observing that the reason is sitting beside you. They are called threads.'

Lucy widened her eyes. 'The threads that bind.'

'Aye, you know of them. Who told you that?'

'Alice, my aunt. She is experienced in travelling but her journeys are intentional. Mine was simply from a stumble, and touching the stone.'

'You said you came at noon, Lucy?' Thelma asked gently.

'Yes. At noon.'

'And the moon?'

Lucy frowned and thought back. It seemed so long ago. 'It was going to be full the day I left because Alice and I had planned to take my little boy out to see the moonrise over Glastonbury Tor that night.'

Tom's voice was anguished. 'The full moon is tonight.'

'So you must journey back today, or you will have to wait another four weeks.'

Lucy looked at Tom and his expression almost broke her heart. 'I can't wait four weeks, Tom. I'm sorry.'

'You say it must be today?' Tom's voice was tight.

'Aye. Today or Lucy will have to wait. The risk of going to the wrong time destination is too great if you stray from the times of the moon. It was great luck that you came to visit me today.' Thelma stood. 'I will leave you to speak. It is two hours until noon. I shall be in the garden. Come out when you decide what you will do.'

Lucy let go of Tom's hand and stood. 'I know what I have to do. I want you to tell me more please, Thelma. I can't afford to stuff this up. I have to go back to the right place and time, to Joshua, my little boy.' She glanced at Tom, but he was looking past her to the window where the stones reared from the field. 'I will follow you out to the garden when I say goodbye to Tom.'

His head flew up. 'No! I'm not going anywhere. We will say our goodbyes as you leave. I will wait here until I know you are safely gone.'

Thelma reached over and squeezed Tom's shoulder before she walked out to the back garden.

Lucy drew a breath and looked back at Tom.

Her heart clenched as she watched a single tear form and roll slowly down his cheek.

'Oh, Tom.' Before she knew it she was sitting in his lap and his arms were around her, his head on her shoulder.

'I'm sorry, Lucy. I was going to be strong, but not having one more night with you to say goodbye has hit hard.'

'I know, sweetheart.' Her hand smoothed his hair, just as she comforted Joshua when he was upset.

'I shall be all right in a moment. It was the shock. I'm sorry, I don't want you to be upset. I want your memory of me to be with a smile on my face looking at you with love.' He sat back and his eyes were clear now.

Lucy cupped his cheeks in her hands. 'I have many memories of you that I will carry in my heart. I will think of you every day of my life, and when I can, I will come back. Please trust me.'

'I will, my love.' He lifted her off his lap, stood and held her close before his lips took hers in the most beautiful kiss of her life. Lucy had no doubt she was loved deeply.

***

One minute before the stroke of noon Tom stood with Lucy at the stones. Her eyes held his as she stepped towards the towering rocks, and he held her right hand tightly, his arm outstretched.

She reached her other hand to the spot where she had touched the cold stone four weeks ago.

'It's time,' Thelma said quietly beside him.

He loosened his hold on Lucy's hand as her eyes stayed on his.

'I love you, Tom. I will see you again.' Her fingers eased away from his and he smiled back at her. 'I promise with all my heart.'

'Safe travels. My love. I will wait for you. I promise with my heart and love.'

Tom tensed as a humming noise engulfed them and they were surrounded by blue light. He put one hand to his head as the noise intensified, and no matter how hard he tried to keep his eyes on Lucy, it was almost impossible to focus. As he watched through his fingers, her body stretched as the blue light covered her in an eerie glow, and then the humming stopped, and she was gone.

His fingers still tingled where he had held her hand, and her face filled his mind. If it hadn't been for her promise to return, he could have quite happily stopped living in that moment.

Slowly he became aware of a warm hand gripping his shoulder. He turned slowly to meet the sympathetic eyes of Thelma McClaren.

'She will be back safely already, lad. Go home and try not to dwell on what you have seen here.'

'May I ask you one question?' His voice was raw, and he cleared his throat as the older woman tipped her head to the side.

'How hard would it be for me to follow her?'

Chapter Twenty-Six

Pilton, United Kingdom - 1989

Lucy closed her eyes as the world faded, and her limbs stretched as though they were being pulled by a huge rubber band. The incessant humming hurt her ears, but she couldn't move her hands to cover them as the blue pulsing light surrounded her. Her body stretched until she thought she couldn't bear it a moment longer, and her vision contracted to a pinpoint of black as a series of images and conversations melded and rushed past her. She fell to the ground and closed her eyes, the grass cool and soothing beneath her cheek.

It was a warm day—the air was pure as she kept her eyes closed and drew in a deep breath. The woods were filled with the sweet sound of birdsong. Behind the birdsong, Lucy slowly became aware of the noise of distant traffic. Opening her eyes, she looked up into a clear blue sky and smiled as a jet stream broke the blue.

'Mummy!'

Her breath caught as a familiar little voice reached her, and she lifted her head.

'Mummy, Mummy. It's my mummy.'

Lucy sat up and watched as Joshua ran across the field towards her. She held her arms open, and love consumed her as her little boy fell into her arms. She rained kisses onto his face and his arms went around her neck.

'Naughty Mummy. You stayed away for a too long time.'

'I got lost, darling, but I'm back now.'

'He missed you, Laura.'

She jumped and stared as Royden appeared beside them. 'Royden? What are you doing here?'

'What do you think? You decide to take off, and Alice had no choice but to call me and tell me that you had gone off on some trip. I'm not happy, but it wasn't fair to leave our son with her. She's not young, you know. I flew over here, and I've missed out on some important meetings. And then you come back and decide to lay around in a field instead of coming home. What the hell is wrong with you?'

If Lucy could have taken Joshua in her arms and gone straight back to where she'd come from, she would have gone without a second thought.

But it was impossible.

Her arms stayed around Joshua, and she didn't look at Royden until Alice spoke over his angry words.

'I told you, Royden. Lucy needed some space and some time on her own. You didn't need to come over here. And just to set the record straight, Lucy, he called to speak to Joshua. I didn't call him.'

'Enough. I'm home now, and everything can go back to normal.'

'Where have you been?' Royden's voice was a tiny bit more pleasant. 'And what the hell are you wearing?'

'Away. Finding myself.' She lifted her chin and stared at him, and pushed up to her feet. Royden didn't help.

'And have you?'

'I have.'

'Well, I'm pleased to hear that. I'll book our flight. Joshua and I are booked on Qantas to Sydney the day after tomorrow. I'll book your seat too.'

Things were happening too fast for Lucy to focus. 'Yes. But wait. We'll talk about it in a while. I want to talk to Alice first.'

Royden, with his usual ability to switch on the charm to get his own way, reached over and kissed her cheek. 'I do want you home, Laura. I missed you. The house is empty without you and Joshua.'

She stared at him, uncertain if he was being honest, or just saying what was expected. 'We'll talk about it later.'

He held her gaze for a moment, and Lucy was surprised that she was devoid of any feeling. No love, no hate, no disappointment. Just a dreadful emptiness.

'Come on, Josh. Let's go see the cows,' Royden said.

'Mummy too?' Joshua held out his little hand.

'You go with Daddy, sweetheart. Aunt Alice and I will catch you up.'

'You *pwomise*?' His little eyes held hers unerringly and a wave of love returned, kicking life into her dull heart.

'I *pwomise*. Now go and see how many cows you can count before I catch you.' She smiled as he took off with a smile towards the stone fence.

'Daddy, lift me up, so I can count the black and white ones.'

Alice came to stand beside her and slipped an arm around her waist. 'Are you all right, dearest Lucy?'

'Sort of.'

'I didn't tell Royden about the stones. I just said you'd gone away for a while when he rang. Before I knew it, he was on the doorstep. He wanted to take Joshua, but I wouldn't let him. It wasn't pleasant, but I stood my ground.'

'I'm so sorry I put you through that, Alice. I fell and I went back. In the blink of an eye, my whole life changed.'

'How far?' Alice asked quietly.

'1851,' Lucy replied when she was sure Royden was too far away to hear. 'I know now what you meant by the threads that bind. I found my love.'

Chapter Twenty-Seven

Violet Cottage, March - 2019

'Oh, Mum, and what happened then?' Beth's eyes glinted with tears.

Lucy put down the blouse she was folding and stared past her daughter, across to the fields where the stones and her future waited.

'I went back to Sydney. I knew that Joshua needed a father—his father—and I tried to make the best of my life. Then when I discovered I was pregnant with you, it was more bearable. I knew then I would always have Tom with me.'

'You didn't ever want to leave and go back to him?'

'Every minute of every day. But equally, at the same time, I wanted to be with you and Joshua just as much. More. As well as wanting to stay, you both *needed* me.'

'Those times we came back to England? Were you tempted to try and go back?'

'Oh, sweetie, you know me so well. That's why I was so cranky each time we were over here. To be so close, and yet so far. And I don't want you to get an inkling of that feeling, because I knew what you'd want to do.'

'What I still want to do. I would like to meet my father.'

'Just let me go, and I will come back and tell you. When I can.'

'As long as it took last time?' Beth frowned.

'No. I'll come back and tell you. It might be a month, it might be a year, but I promise. As soon as I find Tom, or find out what happened, I will come *back* to you.'

'And if you don't I'll *follow* you. I have one question though, Mum. What will you do now if—'

Lucy held one hand up. 'Beth, I made a promise to your father. One that circumstances wouldn't let me keep for many years. But now it's time, and because I took so long, I will just have to face whatever is waiting for me. I'm strong, and I will survive no matter what I find there.'

'I'll worry about you until I see you again.'

Lucy pulled Beth close for a hug. 'I don't want you to. I'm going on an adventure, and this time I know I'm going. I'm prepared.' She gestured to the bag that was packed ready for her journey. She and Beth had raided the vintage stores in town, made some alterations to their purchases and Lucy was satisfied with the clothes she was wearing. She had managed to purchase banknotes and coins from a collectables site—with Beth's help—and hoped she had enough money to last her for a few weeks at least. A soft towel was in her bag, along with four cakes of soap, a tube of toothpaste, and a toothbrush. All of the comforts of home that she remembered she'd missed thirty years ago.

'I love you, Mum,' Beth whispered.

##

Three days later, Lucy tried her best to comfort her daughter as Beth clung to her in the field by the stones. Silas stood to the side and gave them some space.

'It's okay, darling. You know how it works. I'll be fine.'

'Promise me you'll come back because if you don't, I'll come looking, I swear.'

'I've promised, and I'll promise again. Now give me a big hug, wipe your tears, and be happy for me.'

Beth dabbed at her eyes and put her arms around Lucy, and they stood like that for a few moments. Lucy had been to the stone every day for the past few days and memorised the spot she had touched last time. The moon was full tonight and now the sun approached its zenith.

She looked at her watch and reached across to Silas who passed her bag to her.

'I'll see you both soon.' As the humming began, she placed her hand on the exact spot and closed her eyes, waiting to go.

##

Maybe it was being older that made her feel so wretched, but it took Lucy two full days and nights to feel well enough to travel from Glastonbury to St Austell. She'd managed to get herself from the stones to the same hotel that she and Tom had stayed in thirty years before, and slept for two days and nights straight.

When she woke on the morning of the third day, she felt energised and hopeful. Enquiries at the train station revealed that she could now travel direct from Taunton to St Austell and that the train was due to come through Glastonbury in an hour. Lucy purchased a ticket and tried to push back her excitement; the more anticipation she held, the more disappointed she would be if Tom was not there.

Or if he was—no, she couldn't allow herself to think that.

The train trip seemed to take forever, and Lucy sat in a window seat, watching the landscape flash by. As she watched and thought, she made her plan.

It was early evening by the time she disembarked at the train station at St Austell. Lucy's eyes widened. The small township Tom had walked her through thirty years before was now a small city, bustling with crowds and traffic. To the west, in the distance, she could see the white mountains that Beth had found on the internet. She booked into the small hotel adjacent to the railway station and pushed away the doubts that told her she was being foolish. She sat in the dining room and had a bowl of vegetable soup and retired for the night, resisting the strong urge to walk to the cottage where she had spent the month with Tom.

Tomorrow would be soon enough.

Chapter Twenty-Eight

St Austell, June - 1881

Lucy tossed and turned for the whole night. The bed was hard, but that wasn't the reason for her disturbed sleep. Today was the day for which she had waited for more than half her life, and the fear that she wouldn't wake in time had kept her awake. She rose quietly, walked down the hall to the shared bathroom, had a wash, and bound her hair into a French roll. At her throat, she fastened the clasp of the antique brooch she had found in a retro store and straightened the lace collar on her white blouse. Taking a deep breath, she returned to her room, put her notes and coin into the small dilly bag she had packed, and stepped out into the quiet streets of St Austell in June 1881.

First light tinged the dawn sky rose-pink as Lucy made her way towards the harbour. If she found the Harbour House, she could make her way along the clifftop and wait.

Strangely her nervous anticipation had dissipated and a sense of calm had stolen over her.

What will be, will be, she thought.

The streets around the harbour were already busy. Many ships lined the new dock, and harbour sheds and warehouses lined the edge of the water that had once been a rocky foreshore. The sky was getting quite light now, and she hurried up the small path that led to the clifftop. Once she reached the path along the edge, a smile crossed her face. Nothing had changed apart from several wooden benches positioned along the clifftop to take in the view. A golden light began to gild the clouds hovering over the eastern horizon, and she hurried along the path to reach the spot on the cliff overlooking Smuggler's Cove where she had stood with Tom all those years ago.

Lucy stopped and stood at the edge of the path, closing her eyes, recalling the words that had stayed with her.

'Every morning, I shall walk to the cliff, or wherever I am, I will go outside and watch the sunrise, and I will send my love to you over the years.'

'And I will wait to feel it,' she had replied to Tom. And she had felt it every morning of her life.

Happiness filled Lucy as she opened her eyes and watched the first light of the golden orb peep over the horizon. Her fingers went to the porcelain necklace she had never removed. No matter what had happened over the years, she had kept her promise to Tom.

'I came back,' she whispered.

'I knew you would.'

For a moment, Lucy thought the voice was in her head, but her breath caught and held as the words continued. 'Wherever I was, I watched the sunrise as I promised you, and I knew you would come back to me one day.'

She turned slowly.

Tom's familiar beautiful eyes held hers, and the years slipped away. Lucy closed her eyes again briefly as a smile tilted her lips. A face that held so much of Beth, their daughter. Opening them again, she stepped towards Tom as he held his arms wide. The first rays of the sun lit his face as he waited for her, and the love that had stayed with her for the past thirty years surged in her chest.

'Come to me, my love,' he said. 'There will be time for words later.'

'And we have all the time in the world this time, my darling Tom,' Lucy replied before his head blotted out the sunlight and Tom claimed her lips with his.

Epilogue
Pilton, United Kingdom - May, 2019

'Just follow my lead,' Lucy said as she approached the car rental booth next to the train station at Glastonbury. 'And keep your mouth closed,' she added with a laugh.

Tom's eyes had been huge ever since they had come back through the stones. Three days and nights of nonstop talking and loving, in the same cottage that Tom had lived in between his trips to Scandinavia had resulted in them returning through the stones a month later. Tom had spent the days telling her about the last thirty years, how his parents had lived until their seventies, and of his nine nephews and nieces. Lucy had cried when Tom explained how he had told his parents she had died in a carriage accident in London.

'It was the only way I could explain your disappearance as they knew we loved each other.'

He had been amazed that Lucy knew so much about his life and his time in Scandinavia, but his emotion when she had told him about Beth had overcome him.

'I have a child? We have a daughter?'

'We do. And she looks just like you.'

Tom had been bereft of words for so long Lucy had worried he'd had some kind of turn. She had cried when he told her of his parents' deaths, smiled to hear of his brothers' happy marriages and their families, but Tom's reaction to hearing of his daughter had been shock that consumed him.

His response had been unexpected. 'We will go there. Now.'

'We can't go now. We have to wait for the right time. For the cycle of the moon.'

They had waited and while Lucy enjoyed every minute of the time, she knew the month had dragged for Tom, but it had left her secure in the knowledge that she was still loved and that there was a future for them.

Now she signed the car hire agreement, took the keys and led him around the back where the cars were parked.

'Tom, you have to stop looking so wide-eyed at everything and hurry up. At this rate, Beth will have flown back to Australia.'

That was enough for him to jump in the car, once Lucy had shown him how to open the door. The trip from the train station to Violet Cottage took fifteen minutes, and Tom spent the whole trip examining the dashboard instruments and lights.

'Okay. We're here,' she said as she parked in the narrow lane outside the cottage.

Smoke curled lazily from the chimney and as she stepped from the car, Lucy could hear music coming from the back garden.

'I don't want to give Beth too much of a shock, so I'll go around first and prepare her,' she said as they walked along the side path.

'The cottage hasn't changed much, has it?' Tom said as he took her hand.

'No, hardly at all. Just a few mod cons.' Lucy reached up and kissed him. 'Wait here. I won't be long.'

***

Tom stood beside the fence covered in an abundance of fragrant yellow roses. He tapped his foot nervously on the cobbled path, still getting used to the unusual clothes he wore. Lucy had insisted on shopping in Glastonbury after they had spent one night in a hotel, a very different hotel to what he was used to.

Everything about being here fascinated him. Apart from the physical landscape, the world was unrecognisable. The motor vehicles, the square card that Lucy used instead of money, the number of people on the streets and the rush that everyone seemed to be in almost overwhelmed him; it was a pleasure to be standing now in the garden in this quiet, familiar cottage. The same garden where Thelma had comforted him when Lucy had left him. Tom's life had been full, but he had never married. Despite Isabelle Lyndhurst's best efforts, he had waited, trusting that Lucy would come back to him one day.

He looked up as a shadow fell on the path in front of him. A tall girl with dark hair like his stood watching him. Lucy was standing behind her. Tears rolled down her pretty face as she stared at him.

'Beth?' His voice shook.

Lucy stepped forward and took their daughter's hand. 'Beth, come and meet your dad.'

Tom held his arms open and his world shifted as he held his daughter in his arms for the first time.

'Hello, Dad. It's lovely to finally meet you.' Her voice was identical to Lucy's.

'Hello, Beth. It's a great pleasure to meet you too.'

They stood together silently for a long time.

Finally, Tom smiled as he turned to the woman he loved. 'Lucy, now that we have a daughter, I think it's past time we were married. What do you think?'

The sweet smile that spread over her beautiful face had his heart tumbling. 'I think that's a fine idea, Tom.'

Their daughter stepped back and folded her arms. 'I agree, but I have one question. *When* will you get married?'

'Well, that's something we'll have to decide.' Lucy linked one arm through her daughter's and held her hand out to Tom. 'Come and meet Silas, and we'll give Joshua a call and see if they want to travel to a wedding.'

'Travel, Mum?' Beth said. 'To here, or to 1881? I'd rather fancy a visit to my father's house.'

'I think that's something we'll have to decide when Joshua arrives.'

Tom smiled at the two women who were deciding where he would spend his future.

'What do you think, Tom?'

'Wherever you are, I will be, Lucy, my love.'

THE END

Note: Thomas Egbert Adams' death notice does not appear in the *ancestry.com* record in the parish of St Austell in the nineteenth century with that of his parents and brothers, as at the present time he resides in Violet Cottage near the village of Pilton, with his wife, Lucy.

THE THREADS THAT BIND

The other books in the Love Across Time series are all available from Annie's store.
https://www.annieseaton.net/store.html

Megan's story: Book 1-Come Back to Me

Beth's story: Book 2-Follow Me

Lucy's story: Book 3- Finding Home

ANNIE SEATON

Other Books by Annie

Whitsunday Dawn
Undara
Osprey Reef
East of Alice (Nov 22)

Porter Sisters Series

Kakadu Sunset

Daintree

Diamond Sky

Hidden Valley
Larapinta

Augathella Girls Series

Outback Roads

Outback Sky

Outback Escape

Outback Wind

Pentecost Island Series

THE THREADS THAT BIND

Pippa

Eliza

Nell

Tamsin

Evie

Cherry

Odessa

Sienna

Tess

Isla

Sunshine Coast Series

Waiting for Ana

The Trouble with Jack

Healing His Heart

Sunshine Coast Boxed Set

Richards Brother Series

The Trouble with Paradise

ANNIE SEATON

Marry in Haste

Outback Sunrise

Bondi Beach Love Series

Beach House

Beach Music

Beach Walk

Beach Dreams

The House on the Hill

Second Chance Bay Series

Her Outback Playboy

Her Outback Protector

Her Outback Haven

Her Outback Paradise

The McDougalls of Second Chance Bay Boxed Set

Love Across Time Series

Come Back to Me

THE THREADS THAT BIND

Follow Me

Finding Home

The Threads that Bind

Others

Deadly Secrets

Adventures in Time

Silver Valley Witch

The Emerald Necklace

Worth the Wait

Ten Days in Paradise

Follow the Sun (May 22)

Secrets of River Cottage (Nov 22)

About the Author

Annie lives in Australia, on the beautiful north coast of New South Wales. She sits in her writing chair and looks out over the tranquil Pacific Ocean. She writes contemporary romance and loves telling the stories that always have a happily ever after. She lives with her very own hero of many years and they share their home with Toby, the naughtiest dog in the universe, and Barney, the rag doll kitten, who hides when the four grandchildren come to visit.

Stay up to date with her latest releases at her website: http://www.annieseaton.net

If you would like to stay up to date with Annie's releases, subscribe to her newsletter here:
http://www.annieseaton.net

Awards

Book of the Year (Whitsunday Dawn) - Ausrom Readers' Choice Awards 2018.

Finalist (Whitsunday Dawn) – ARRA romantic suspense.

Finalist - NZ KORU award 2018 and 2020.

Winner - Best Established Author of the Year 2017 AUSROM.

Longlisted - Sisters in Crime Davitt Awards 2016, 2017, 2018, 2019.

Finalist (Kakadu Sunset) - Book of the Year, Long Romance, RWA Ruby awards 2016.

Winner - Best Established Author of the Year 2015 AUSROM.

Winner - Author of the Year 2014 AUSROM.

Printed in Dunstable, United Kingdom